S0-BAQ-602

PIECES OF
THE PICTURE

PIECES OF
THE PICTURE

Barbara M. Joosse

J. B. Lippincott   New York

First Edition

Library of Congress Cataloging-in-Publication Data
Joosse, Barbara M.
    Pieces of the Picture / by Barbara M. Joosse. — 1st ed.
        p.   cm.
    Summary: Deeply resentful of having to move from Chicago
to rural Wisconsin after her father's death, teenage Emily
struggles to understand her seemingly calm, hard-working mother
and to come to terms with her own mixed emotions.
    ISBN 0-397-32342-5 : $
    ISBN 0-397-32343-3 (lib bdg.) : $
    [1. Mothers and daughters—Fiction.   2. Grief—Fiction.
3. Wisconsin—Fiction.]   I. Title.
PZ7.J7435Pi 1989   88-28151
[Fic]—dc 19   CIP
                                                          AC

For Gary and Edna

Contents

CHAPTER ONE

Looking In

Emily crouched low in the porch swing, hanging her feet over the porch railing. A windless, icy drizzle stung at her bare ankles. "Typical," she thought, pulling her jacket more tightly around her. This was the kind of weather she'd come to expect in Ellison Bay. Emily glared into the miserable mist. She couldn't see much from the porch except the hazy outline of the gazebo, which floated somewhere inside the mist like an unanchored, unmanned ship. But Emily wouldn't have seen much anyway. This was Ellison Bay.

It was Friday, after school, and Emily had already had a rotten day. Now it was getting worse. Emily looked over her shoulder, narrowing her eyes against the light coming from the living room window. Inside, a sturdy fire warmed Mother and seven guests. They were laughing and gorging themselves on birthday cake. Emily pulled her bare fists into her coat sleeves. She felt like the Little Matchgirl.

Emily watched Mother lift the tray to pass around the birthday cake—the one she, Mother, had made for herself. Mother offered the tray to Mr. Ganopolis. Mr. Ganopolis was bald, except for an anemic little fringe at the bottom. He had let some of the fringe grow very long so he could swoop it up over the bald spot. Mr. Ganopolis had arrived yesterday afternoon. He slept in Room 7. Emily knew that because she'd had to carry his bag for him. He also snored in Room 7. Emily knew *that* because she'd listened at his door.

Emily cocked her ear toward the living room window. She leaned as far as she could in that direction without allowing her face to show above the porch swing. She could only hear muted sounds—no real words. Still, she could imagine the conversation inside very well:

"Care for more cake, Mr. Ganopolis?"

"No, no, dear. I've had quite enough."

"Oh, do have another piece. My only pleasure in this life is serving all of you."

Mr. Ganopolis was, indeed, taking another

2

piece. Emily had known he would. Now Sara Mueller was holding her coffee cup in the air. She probably wants a wee drop more. No. She's making a toast, thought Emily, disgusted. Emily watched through the old, ripply glass while Ms. Mueller stood in front of the fireplace, holding up her cup. She turned to toast Mother, exposing her back to Emily.

Ms. Mueller's skirt was pulled tightly across her ample rear end, causing the fabric to bunch up at the waistband in two rolls. Her white slip sagged beneath her skirt. Ms. Mueller's legs looked like sausages. At the ends of her legs were red, plasticky shoes.

If I looked like that, thought Emily, I'd wear a sack over my entire body.

Mother bowed her head, graciously accepting the birthday toast. The rest of the guests raised their cups.

"To Agnes!" Emily could hear them through the window.

"To Agnes!"

After everyone's cup was drained, Mother took the cups, one by one, and filled them from the large pot on the sideboard. Then the group started to sing. This was too much! Emily swung around and focused on the sign. The sign, innocent enough with its careful blue lettering, stood for all her family had come to, and Emily hated it. The Ellison Inn. The Ellison Inn was in Ellison Bay, at the end of Door County, which was on the edge of Wisconsin, which was at the end of nowhere. The earth ended after Ellison Bay. The civilized earth ended before it.

Emily thought of her life in two acts: Act One, her childhood, was set in a stylish brownstone in a trendy section of Chicago. The outfits in Act One were colorful and cute. There were many characters in Act One, and all of them liked Emily. In Act One, Emily had a father.

Act Two was this. Emily and Mother alone in Ellison Bay. Daddy dead. No money. Mother running Mor and Far's home as an inn.

Emily wished she had known that her only happiness would be in the first twelve years of her life. She would have appreciated it more.

Emily drew her long legs from the railing and planted them on the porch floor. Emily was tall for her age. When she was younger, Emily had been adorable—everybody said so. Emily felt she had done adorable very well. Her blond hair had enough curl to be bouncy, and Daddy had seen to it that she had darling clothes. Also, she had had a way of leveling adults with her green eyes that made them think she was mentally advanced for her age.

After twelve, Emily wasn't "cute" anymore. When she slipped a swear word into a sentence, it wasn't amusing. When she used her leveling look, teachers thought she was being defiant. As if that weren't bad enough, her body was going off in two directions as if it had a split personality. Her legs were growing faster than her top. Emily had these long, skinny legs that made every kind of pantyhose in the world bag at the calf. Her top half was shorter than her bottom half and she had two little warty things that looked more like blemishes than breasts. She felt like one of those animal flip books where you could put the top of an ape on the bottom of a giraffe. At least she didn't have zits.

Well. Now she was hungry. She should have eaten more at dinner, but she had made the mistake of joining the guests at the dining room table instead of taking a tray into her room. And the sound of all their voices, flying across the table like sharp fragments of glass, had driven her away. So she'd only eaten firsts.

Emily brushed away some of the water with hands that glowed ghostly white in the light from the living room. When she walked toward the door, her wet sneakers squeaked on the wooden floor. Emily opened the door. Inside, the cheerful voices hit her like a fist.

". . . It's been years since I've been to a birthday party," burbled Mr. Ganopolis.

". . . didn't bring a present, but I didn't know," said Kyle Joseph.

". . . I found the cutest little shop in Fish Creek," said Laura Halsley. "I'll take you tomorrow."

"Emily!" said Mother, looking up at Emily.

The talking stopped. Eight people, sixteen eyes, stared at Emily. She felt naked. She wished she *were* naked. That would give them something to talk about, something colorful to remember about their trip to Door County.

"Hello, dear," said Mrs. Sharples, smiling carefully at Emily. "Come in and have some of your mother's birthday cake."

Emily dripped on the wooden floor. She looked at the piece left on the sideboard. It was one with a rose. It would be a grand gesture to refuse it, hungry as she was. But before she had a chance, Mother had whisked the piece off the sideboard, added a fork, and placed it in Emily's hands. Mother's empty hands fluttered in the air for an instant. She shoved them in her apron pockets. Then she reached out toward Emily. "Emily, I . . ."

Emily wasn't sure if Mother was going to strike her or stroke her. Perhaps Mother was unsure also. Her hands remained in front of Emily's face for several anxious seconds.

"Why, you're soaking wet!" she said, her hands finally coming to life as they jerked to Emily's shoulder. Mother brushed away the water.

"Happy birthday, Mother," mumbled Emily without looking up. Emily quickly shoved cake into her mouth, choking down all the words that were jammed in her throat.

Mother waited, her hands back in her apron pockets, until Emily scraped the last of the frosting from the plate. Then she turned, gathered the dirty dishes from each guest, and stacked them on the sideboard. The party was over.

Emily left what she called the "visual traffic pattern," and disappeared behind the oak registration desk. The visual traffic pattern is the area most likely to be watched. People's eyes usually follow a predictable path—like around a table or sitting area, or between two moving objects. If you left the visual traffic pattern you were not likely to be noticed.

Mother returned for another armload of dirty dishes, which she carried into the kitchen. Other people's dirty dishes were disgusting. Emily thought of little splatterings of saliva and hair left on the plates. When Mother made Emily help with guest dishes, she always wore rubber gloves.

Emily peeled the cellophane from a root-beer barrel. Nothing much was happening in the living room. Emily didn't really expect anything dramatic, but you could tell a lot from small clues. Emily liked to keep an eye on things.

This wasn't always so. Back home—her real home in Chicago, not here—Emily was so busy she didn't have time to gawk at other people. She was, in fact, the third most popular girl at University Prep School. But Door County—at least during the off-season from September through June—was full of hicks. And hicks didn't appreciate Emily's wit and fashion inventiveness. So, with little else to do, Emily had taken to snooping.

Kyle Joseph lit Beth Thomas's cigarette, a Virginia Slim.

Aha! There's something interesting. Emily pulled a small spiral notebook from her sweatshirt pocket. Beth's fingertips brushed Kyle's hand as he held the flame to her cigarette. Then she inhaled the smoke, held it, and exhaled slowly.

Emily wrote: *Kyle J. and Beth T.—developing love interest. Virginia Slim.*

The kitchen door swung open and Mother gathered the last of the dishes. Mother's hair, mostly brown with a recent shot of gray, had one deep wave that wound around her head. After the wave, her hair dropped feebly to her neck. Mother's neck was long and slender, like a dancer's. Her shoulders, under the turtleneck, were sharp and defined.

Mr. Ganopolis turned and headed for the stairs. The other guests were making ready-to-go movements as well. The registration desk was between the living room and the stairway, so Emily would soon be in the visual traffic pattern. She put her notebook back in her sweatshirt pocket along with a handful of candy. Then she slipped from behind the desk, through Mother's bedroom to the little cottage behind the inn—her room.

Emily pulled the key from around her neck and unlocked the door. She groped for the light switch and flicked it, lighting the bare bulb above her bed. The room was sparsely furnished. It contained a bed and dresser, two posters thumbtacked to the plywood walls and a turquoise metal fifties chair with partially rusted legs. Mother had used all their Chicago furniture plus all the furniture from Mor and Far's house, when she turned this place into an inn. In fact, she had had to buy

Emily's bed frame, box-spring, and mattress, an expense Mother probably resented because now they were so poor.

Now Emily spread out the candy on her bed, along with the notebook. The harsh glare of the bare bulb above Emily's bed brought the whole thing into focus. She stared at six pieces of candy and one entry in a notebook. This was the bounty of her day. This was all Emily had to show for having lived this day in this place. She lifted up the notebook and began to write:

> *Today is Mother's birthday. If Daddy were here we would still be in Chicago, probably out for dinner, probably at Pinky's. Mother would have two presents, one from me, one from Daddy. She would wait until dessert to open them. Daddy's would have been expensive and Mother would have scolded him for spending so much money. I'm not sure what mine would have been. I never know what to get Mother. Daddy would have helped me pick it out.*
>
> *I didn't get Mother a present this year but next year I will.*

Emily sat on the bed cross-legged, her arms hanging at her sides. The contrast between what today would have been and what it really was settled like a stone in her stomach.

Daddy had been her pal. Daddy had bought Emily her first pantyhose and her own telephone. When she was six, Daddy had taken her to Marshall Field's to get her ears pierced and bought her diamond studs. Then he'd taken Emily home on the back of his motorcycle.

Mother had been furious. She spoke, as always, with quiet control, but her lips were pulled into tight white ridges, so Emily knew she was angry.

"Tom! Why must you always be so irresponsible? Emily is too young to have pierced ears! She'll never keep them clean."

This was untrue. Emily did keep her ears clean.

"And she's *far* too young to have diamond studs. We can't afford it!"

But Daddy laughed and squeezed Emily's hand. "Well, it's too late to plug up the holes," he said. "Besides, I think diamond earrings make Emily look zarky." Zarky was Daddy and Emily's word for great-looking.

Mother started to say something else but Daddy kissed her. Every time she was about to speak, Daddy stopped her with a kiss. The argument was over.

Emily reached up to her ear and felt the little hole with her finger. Then she scraped up her candy and notebook and walked barefooted across the linoleum floor to her dresser. She put the candy and notebook on top, opened the top drawer, and took the diamond studs from their box. Emily twisted them in her fingers, admiring the way they took the cold light-bulb light and made it hot and fiery. She slipped them into her ears. Then she pulled out Daddy's old Chicago Bears T-shirt. It was his "Saturday shirt." In the beginning, right after Daddy died, Emily liked to smell it when she put it on. But eventually Mother insisted on washing it. Then Daddy's smell was gone. After that, Emily held her nose when she put it on so she wouldn't notice.

Emily walked to the door. There was only one light switch in the guest house, and that was next to the door. Emily turned off the light and returned to her bed in the dark. There, she crawled under the covers and tried to sleep. But she could not. There were many nights now when Emily couldn't fall asleep. That was when pictures crowded into Emily's closed eyes. Sometimes the pictures were of Daddy. Sometimes they were of old friends. Sometimes they were pictures of guests or Ellison Bay hicks laughing and having fun without her.

Tonight they were pictures of Mother. Emily had seen paintings of clowns with smiling mouths and crying eyes at craft fairs. That was how Mother looked tonight, laughing and singing along with the guests. But there was something behind her eyes that wasn't happy. Mother would never be happy. Just as some people are born to live a life of luxury or adventure or joy, Mother was born to live a life of dullness and work. She was born an old woman, probably forty. It was a medical miracle. Emily thought of the headline: WOMAN GIVES BIRTH TO FORTY-YEAR-OLD BABY! It would have been funny if it weren't painfully true.

CHAPTER TWO

The Sealed Door

Emily woke up when she heard the honking. The first time she had heard the geese Emily had thought they were dogs barking, an understandable mistake, considering she was a city kid. But one day she looked up and saw them heading south, honking like crazy.

Emily plopped her pillow over her head, burying her face in the mattress. Forget it. She was not getting up early on Saturday. Sleeping in was one luxury that didn't cost money.

I wonder where the geese are going, she thought. She'd heard of Horicon Marsh, near Milwaukee, a sort of goose motel. She wondered if all the Door County geese gathered there. She wondered if some poor widow and her child ran the place there. And how did the geese figure out the travel route? She could hear them arguing now. "It's Herb's turn to lead." "No way." "You were supposed to turn west at the lake." "The map says east." "I have to go to the bathroom." "When are we going to be there?"

It was no use. Emily couldn't get back to sleep. Now she was faced with a long Saturday. There was no one to hang around with. There was no place to go. She was too old to watch cartoons. Emily stood on her bed and pulled aside the plaid bedspread that covered her window. She watched the geese, now nearly out of sight. She wished she were going along.

The geese were flying low because of the cloud cover. She knew about the cloud cover because Emily heard Kyle Joseph spouting off about it yesterday. He was trying to impress Beth Thomas with his knowledge of wildlife. Apparently she'd been impressed. She'd let him light her cigarette last night.

Emily took off Daddy's Saturday shirt. She instinctively covered her chest, a gesture she'd adopted when other girls had started developing breasts while she'd been developing chest blemishes.

Then she put on a sweatsuit, no socks, and

tennis shoes. She pinned a funky rhinestone poodle on her sweatsuit. She would never let the stodginess of Ellison Bay overcome her sense of style.

Emily sat cross-legged on her bed and wrote a list:

Saturday
1. *Get dressed.*
2. *Listen at guest doors.*
3. *Eat breakfast.*

Emily checked off the first item, then made another list. She titled it "How I would spend a million dollars if I won a lottery."

1. *Buy a lot of clothes and jewelry, including a diamond bracelet which I would wear with jeans ($25,000).*
2. *Buy a big-screen color television for my room ($2,000).*
3. *Get a new room, decorated ($20,000).*
4. *Get a Rolls-Royce, silver, and hire a chauffeur to drive me to dumb Gibraltar School.*

Emily crossed out number four. She wrote:

4. *Attend a boarding school on the East Coast somewhere. Tuition, $20,000 per year × 5 years = $100,000.*

Emily added that up. It totaled $147,000. She had $853,000 left to spend. Probably it would be a good idea to invest it, she thought. That way, I could be rich for the rest of my life. So she wrote:

5. *Invest $850,000.*
6. *Buy Mother new clothes, $3,000.*

It was wet and damp outside, heavy, like it was going to snow. Mrs. Sharples had said she hoped it would, and had brought her cross-country skis just in case. Fat chance she would actually use them, even if it did snow. Emily had examined her skis. They were brand-new.

Mrs. Sharples was a couch potato. She'd never actually skied, Emily was sure. She just talked like she did. She was probably one of those people who left a needlepoint tennis cover in her car all summer to make people think she was a tennis nut and belonged to a club or something. Emily would have to check out her stuff for evidence. Emily was, after all, a reasonable person. If Mrs. Sharples had a park sticker on her car window or a lift ticket stapled to her jacket, Emily would be the first to admit her mistake.

She climbed the stairs slowly, adjusting her weight to absorb the creaks. Mother kept all the linens on the unoccupied third floor. Emily needed a stack of towels for her "cover." The third floor was nearly as large as the second floor. There were several rooms and a long hallway. Some of the rooms were filled with pieces of broken furniture. Most were just filled with dust.

Emily spent many hours in the small end room, the one that led to an airing porch. The room smelled like dry, withered paper and had three large windows, and the combination of dust and sunlight seemed a comforting contrast. Also, the room contained a sealed door. Emily walked there now and yanked at the door. It was sealed with some kind of hardened foam and was impossible to open without making a big deal of it. Emily didn't know why it was sealed. Was there a dead body in there? Or maybe a murder weapon? Maybe it had been a love nest many years ago and now it was sealed from tender eyes. Maybe it was haunted.

Emily knew the real contents could never be as interesting as she imagined. That's why she'd never actually gone through the fuss of opening it. Still, she was drawn to the room time after time. She leaned her forearm against the sealed door and rested her head there. It left a dusty mark on her sweatshirt. Then she walked to the linens room, picked up a stack of towels, and began her rounds.

Emily crept along the second floor hall to Room 1, Laura Halsley's room, and listened at the door. When she heard the bed creak softly she moved on to Room 2, Sara Mueller's. Emily heard the snap of an old-fashioned suitcase opening and she heard Ms. Mueller open the window. Ms. Mueller seemed to like fresh air, not caring a bit that it cost a fortune to heat the place and that Emily could have used the heating money to buy a small television for her room. Ms. Mueller walked heavily toward the door. Emily busied herself with the stack of towels.

Swoosh. The door opened, revealing Ms. Mueller, whose face, without makeup, resembled Play-Doh. Her bosom—other women had breasts, Ms. Mueller had a bosom—was stuffed into a pink quilted wraparound robe. She smelled like dentures.

"Uh." Ms. Mueller cleared her throat. "Why, hello, uh . . ."

"Emily."

"Ah, yes. Emily. You're up early this morning, aren't you, dear?"

"As you can see," Emily said, showing her the towels, "I have work to do."

"Yes, well, I'm sure that you do. It's nice to see young people working."

"That's me," said Emily. "Work work work."

"Carry on, then," Ms. Mueller said, clutching the top of her robe with one hand. Then she waggled down the hall toward the bathroom, her terry-cloth slippers slapping the wooden floors as she went.

Emily stuffed one of the towels in the back of her sweatsuit pants. "It's nice to see young people working," she mumbled, clutching her sweatshirt top across her bosom as she waggled down the hall to Room 4.

It would be the most horrible thing to be as fat as Sara Mueller. Emily decided to eat only three muffins for breakfast.

Room 3 was unoccupied. Room 4 was occupied by Beth Thomas. Emily couldn't hear a thing in Room 4. She stuck her ear right up to the door. Still, not a sound. Very suspicious. Mr. and Mrs. Sharples had left Room 5 early this morning. Emily supposed it was safe for Mrs. Sharples to get up early as long as there was no snow and she couldn't ski anyway. Then she could cluck about what a shame it was that there wasn't any snow and how truly she hoped they would have a good season.

Mr. Ganopolis was snoring up a storm in Room 7.

Before Emily got to Kyle Joseph's room, she heard the bathroom door open. Emily had forgotten to take the towel out of her pants! It would be difficult to explain to Ms. Mueller, who was sure to ask about it—*"Would you care to explain to me, dear, why you have a towel stuffed in your pants?"* She'd have to come back and listen at Kyle's door later. Emily walked down the back hallway. She pulled the towel out of her pants, put the stack of towels on the landing, and walked downstairs.

Apple muffins for breakfast today, thought Emily, sniffing cinnamon. Mother walked quickly toward the kitchen. She was thrust forward, as if the extra few inches would get her to the kitchen faster. A small timer was clipped to her waist, peeping. Mother groped at her waist to find the off button.

"Mother," called Emily, sitting on the bottom step.

Peep peep peep peep. Silence.

"Mother," Emily called again. Mother turned around.

"Yes, Emily?"

"I'd like a tray this morning."

"Fine, dear," said Mother. "I'll have it ready in a few minutes."

Emily picked up a fashion magazine from the coffee table and dropped into the blue striped chair. She thumbed through the issue, back to front. Why, she wondered, don't magazines print from back to front? Everyone reads them that way. If Daddy were still alive, she'd mention it to him. Daddy had been an advertising executive. Very important. Clients listened to what he had to say. Daddy said Emily was the Quintessential Consumer. So he listened to what *she* had to say. When Emily said, "I think there should be secret code rings in cereal boxes instead of tic-tac-toe games," Daddy saw to it that there were. When Emily said, "I would buy more bubble gum if it came with little scratch-and-sniff stickers on the outside to match the flavor on the inside," Daddy went to Bubble Wonderful and told them. Bubble Wonderful thought the idea was brilliant, and Daddy had a new account. Daddy and Emily made a great team.

Emily thought Daddy should have been rich, with all the good ideas they had. Mother said he would have been if he'd been the least bit careful with their money. She said he spent every dime he ever made, and then some. She said if he'd bought life insurance instead of nonsense they wouldn't be poor now. Then, when Mor and Far died, leaving their home to Mother in their will, she wouldn't have had to run it as an inn. Emily thought those were hateful things for Mother to say. As if it was Daddy's fault that he had died. As if Mother hadn't enjoyed all the things Daddy had bought for them.

Mrs. Sharples burst through the front door, Mr. Sharples in tow. Emily slid lower into the chair so they wouldn't talk to her. She heard Mrs. Sharples rubbing her hands together. "It's an extremely cold day, Ernie," she said, unzipping her jacket, "for November. I've . . ."

"Yes, it's cold," said Ernie, managing to get in three words before Mrs. Sharples nattered on. The Sharpleses walked toward the dining room table.

Emily pulled out her notebook. She wrote: *Ernie Sharples—three words.*

Normally, three words wouldn't have been a big deal and Emily wouldn't have bothered to write it down. But from Ernie Sharples it was like the Gettysburg Address, and Emily wanted it on record.

Emily looked over the top of the chair at the

23

dining room table. The Sharpleses were there, along with Laura Halsley, Mr. Ganopolis, and Sara Mueller. Ms. Mueller looked better with makeup. Emily headed toward the kitchen, carrying her magazine. "Is my tray ready?" she asked.

"Yes, Emily," Mother called over her shoulder, gesturing at the tray with her chin. Mother was pouring coffee into a thermos. Two filled thermoses were on the counter, along with a platter of muffins and a bowl of vegetable scrambled eggs.

Emily lifted the red-checked napkin from the top of the tray. There were four muffins, five pats of butter, and a plate of scrambled eggs. Emily took out one of the muffins and put it on the counter. "I don't have any juice," she reminded Mother. Mother set the percolator down and opened the refrigerator. She pulled a juice pitcher out and closed the door with her foot.

"Sorry, dear," she said. Mother poured juice into a small blue glass and handed it to Emily. "Can you manage?"

"Yes," said Emily, tucking the magazine under her arm, then picking up the tray.

"Oh, Mother . . . ?"

"Yes?"

"What's in the sealed room, the one on the third floor?" Emily hadn't intended to ask Mother—she really didn't know why she had.

Mother poured cream into a little pitcher with one eye on the clock. "Fine, dear," she answered absentmindedly.

Fine? Apparently Mother hadn't heard what Emily asked, so Emily took advantage of Mother's preoccupation. "Then it's okay if I open the door and look inside?"

"Uh-huh." Mother put sugar in a bowl.

"And then it's okay to buy a pair of French-cut jeans."

"Uh-huh."

"Which I'll do right after I shovel elephant dung in India."

"Uh-huh . . . what?"

"Never mind, Mother. Just a little joke."

Emily swung through the kitchen door, leaving Mother at the counter, dazed. She walked through the dining room. "There was a time," she thought, angrily, "when Mother listened to everything I said." Emily walked through Mother's bedroom toward the cottage. She put her breakfast things down on Mother's dresser to rearrange her load. That's when she heard Mrs. Sharples.

"Can you believe that child?" she said. "I swear she doesn't do a thing around here. She sits on her duff and lets her mother do all the work."

"I don't know," said Sara Mueller. "She was doing something with a towel this morning."

"She was up to no good, if you ask me," said Mrs. Sharples.

Well, thought Emily, I didn't ask you. Emily's eyes stung and her hands trembled. She gathered her breakfast things and went through the back door to her cottage. But she had no appetite. She pulled the paper off one of the muffins and stared into her juice. She hated everything about her life. She hated being poor. She hated being lonely. Emily figured lonely and poor went together. She knew she should help Mother more. But it wasn't her fault they were poor. She never wanted to come here in the first place.

Why did Daddy have to die? If someone had to die, why couldn't it have been Mother? But Mother never would have ridden a motorcycle. If she had, she would have been wearing a helmet and a safety harness or something and would have gone twelve miles an hour. Mother was stodgy, like Ellison Bay. She was careful and efficient and responsible. Emily thought the timer on Mother's waist was the perfect accessory. She was a clock watcher—always on time, always responsible.

Emily looked at her breakfast tray. While she was thinking, she had crumbled the muffins into a million pieces and shredded the paper wrappers. Well, she wasn't hungry anyway. Emily opened the door and threw the crumbs outside for the birds. She heard a car start. Emily looked up and saw it was Beth Thomas. Beth was only scheduled to stay Friday night but Emily had thought she might stay longer, considering the romantic development. Apparently not.

Beth got out, leaving the motor running. Her car was a red Alpha Romeo with Illinois license plates. Beth lived in Chicago. Emily pulled out her notebook and quickly wrote: *Emily Ruth Crockett*. Then she tore out the paper, folded it several times, and ran to Beth Thomas's car. She slid it in a corner of the trunk where Beth would not be likely to see it. The note would travel south, to Chicago. It would be like a piece of Emily still lived there.

Kyle came out with Beth, carrying her suitcase. They were talking, their faces nearly touching. Beth shook her hair, laughing up at Kyle. Kyle put the suitcase in Beth's car and closed the trunk. He reached around Beth and pulled her close.

Then they kissed a long, juicy kiss full of animal passion and true romance.

Emily wondered if anyone would ever kiss her like that. It didn't look as if she would ever be beautiful, like Beth. And even if she was, who would find her out here in Ellison Bay?

"You're sure you have to go to that meeting?" Kyle's arm was still around Beth's shoulders. He kissed her again.

"Mmm. I wish I didn't have to."

"Well then, I'll call," promised Kyle.

"I'll answer," said Beth. She slid into the car, closed the door, and drove off with Emily's paper in the trunk.

CHAPTER THREE

Open!

The paring knife was the most useful tool. Emily had tried a pick, a chisel, and a small screwdriver, but the knife was thin enough to slide in the door crack and pick at the white, foamy stuff that held the door tight. Emily had been working on the knotty-pine door for more than an hour. And now, finally, the door swung free. It was dark inside with only the thin light from the other room to give shape to the shadows. But Emily could see the room was not empty. She ran her hand along the wall for a light switch. There was none.

As Emily's eyes became accustomed to the dark, she noticed a bare bulb in the center of the room. Maybe it had a string switch. She spread her hands in front of her and groped toward the middle of the room. If there was a dead body, she hoped it was not between the door and the light bulb. Under the bulb, Emily swung her arms over her head until she felt a string brush her right forearm. She grabbed it, pulled, and was immediately blinded by the light.

Emily shaded her eyes from the glare and focused on a dark corner of the room. There she saw a full-length oval mirror, a chest of drawers, and some hatboxes. This was an attic, full of stuff!

There were old steamer trunks, a brown horsehair couch, a Victrola, books, and old newspapers. There were two portraits of Mor and Far that looked at Emily with obvious disapproval. Emily stared back at them. She'd never seen a picture of her grandparents—or even Mother as a girl. Mor and Far didn't approve of such things. Apparently, though, an oil portrait was okay. Emily covered the portraits with a dusty sheet. She didn't want these harsh people looking at her as she snooped into their things.

Emily opened one of the steamer trunks, a big one with a curved top. *Hans Thorgeson, New York Harbor*, was written on the front in spidery script. This must be one of the trunks Far had brought when he came from Norway! Inside were old clothes. There were two of Far's sea captain's hats and some heavy wool Norwegian sweaters. There were pipes and sturdy wool pants. Emily pulled the pants over her sweats and rolled them up at the bottom. The pants were very long, and she had to roll them up several times. Now she knew who was responsible for her gangly legs! She slipped a sweater over her head—it was hot and itchy at the neck—and stuck a pipe in her mouth and a hat on her head. She swaggered over to the oval mirror.

"Aye, matey," she said to her reflection. Emily cocked her leg and smiled at her reflection. The too-big clothes made her look smaller, almost frail. Set against the dark clothing, her short blond hair looked even lighter, tousled and . . . boyish. She looked like a young boy running off to sea! She knew she was quite a contrast to Far's dark, forbidding face. His nose was thin and long. Hers was the same shape but much shorter. Far's skin was ruddy, as though it had been whipped by the winds to a rough red, and his eyes were the deep blue of Lake Michigan. Emily's skin was fair and her eyes were pale blue. It was almost as if she were a lighter, softer version of Far.

Emily peeled back the sheet from Far's portrait. Far had bushy, thundering brows and tightly ridged lips—no wonder Mother had been afraid of him. Emily didn't remember Far very well. He was old when Emily was born, and he had died when she was a little girl. But she didn't have warm memories of the man. She liked the smell of him, she remembered that. He smelled of cherry pipe tobacco. But Far was stiff. His lap was hard. And Emily remembered that he didn't like chocolate ice cream.

She also remembered how nervous and bossy Mother was before Mor and Far came to visit. The house was always clean, but it was spotless before they came. Emily uncovered Mor's portrait. Yes. This was a spotlessly clean woman. Emily *did* remember Mor. She had died right after Daddy. She died, Emily knew, of heart trouble. The trouble was, Emily figured, she didn't have one.

Mor was stern and thrifty. She was the only person Emily ever knew who saved leftover salad and made people eat it. Mor made soup every Saturday out of all the leftovers from the week. No matter what it was, it went into the soup. Whenever Emily ate Mor's soup she figured it was as disgusting as soup could get.

No wonder this place was so full. It was like Mor's soup, a lifetime full of leftovers. But unlike Mor's soup, this place was not full of disgusting food, it was full of treasures. There were dozens of trunks and boxes. Just *think* what must be inside some of them! Each one held a mystery, sealed to the world, maybe for decades. And Emily would be the one to uncover the secrets, like an archeologist in a pharaoh's tomb.

This was the best thing that had happened to Emily in Ellison Bay. It was exciting and suspenseful—a real contrast to her dismal life, and Emily decided to make it last as long as she could. If she opened just one box a day, she could make the whole thing last for weeks. That would give her something to look forward to, something to think about when things got bad.

Emily took off Far's clothes, folded them carefully, and returned them to the chest. She snapped the trunk shut and pulled out her notebook. She wrote:

Item 1—Steamer trunk. Far's sea clothes.
I have discovered the mystery behind the sealed door. It is an Attic. Every box, every trunk, every piece of furniture holds some small clue that will uncover the hidden secrets of the Thorgeson Family.

I look more like Far than I thought. Would he have looked like me if he had been a girl?

Emily closed her notebook, pulled the light string, and left.

Downstairs, Emily filed her fingernails at the dining room table. Beth's fingernails were immaculate. Emily knew hers could use a little work.

Mother and Ms. Mueller were in the kitchen shredding cabbage for cole slaw. Emily could hear every word they said. "Sara, I can't thank you enough for giving me a hand," Mother said.

"Glad to do it. I didn't have a thing to do today but read anyway, and I'm happy to have the company," Ms. Mueller said.

There were several minutes of silence before Mother said, "So . . ." "So" came out croaky. Mother cleared her throat. "So, Sara, you were a teacher?"

"Yes, for forty years. I'm an old-maid schoolteacher."

Emily blew the filing dust from her fingernails. Her nails were even and rounded. They looked pretty good.

Mother said, "But a good one. I'll bet you made a good teacher."

Emily opened the bottle of Iris Pink fingernail polish and began to put it on her fingernails.

"I did," Ms. Mueller said. "I have to say I was a very fine teacher. Why, the school had a retirement party for me and two hundred of my old students returned to Grafton for the banquet. Some were bankers and teachers and scientists. One was a senator!"

"Really!"

"But now I'm retired, of course. I miss it, teaching."

"Do you do a lot of traveling?"

"Some. But the children were my family. Now my days seem so useless. Pointless. You have a daughter, Agnes. And you're so busy you don't have time to breathe! Maybe you don't know what I mean."

"But I do, Sara! I'm busy all day, it's true. But I usually feel the whole day has passed and I haven't done anything really useful." Mother's voice sounded thick. "The work never ends, Sara. I never get ahead. And worse, Emily and I seem so distant. She's my own daughter, Sara, but she feels so far away. I just don't know," Mother said vaguely.

Emily held her nails out. It wasn't exactly a professional manicure, but it wasn't bad. She

35

walked to her room, thinking about what Mother had said.

Dinner was uneventful. Guests. Emily. Home-cooked food. Cole slaw. White dinner rolls with little pats of butter. Polite conversation, except, of course, for Mrs. Sharples.

"I see Mr. Ganopolis left us," she said.

"Why, yes," Ms. Mueller said. "He left this morning."

"I don't suppose he could afford to stay longer," Mrs. Sharples said, leaning over the table toward Ms. Mueller. "He had his own company, you know. Manufactured tractor parts. The thing went belly-up and he had to file for bankruptcy." Mrs. Sharples eyes were narrow. Her voice was hard and raspy. "I suppose our Mrs. Crockett will be lucky to get paid for his stay here—the man hasn't got a dime." Mrs. Sharples nodded her chin self-righteously and began to cut her pork chop.

After a while, Mrs. Sharples continued, "Somebody looks a little down-in-the-mouth to-night," and she nodded at Kyle. "That lovely Beth Thomas left this morning, didn't she?"

Kyle's ears grew pink. He didn't say anything.

Emily wasn't sure when the honking started. It was a soft, continuous honking, so it became background noise, and Emily wasn't conscious of it for a long time. Eventually, like a lot of small drips that finally reach the top of the sink, she noticed. The honking seemed close. It seemed to contain many voices.

"Excuse me," said Emily, pushing away from the table. She left behind a half-eaten pork chop, along with dessert.

When she stepped outside, the honking surrounded her. In the dark, it was difficult to figure out where it was coming from. Emily walked slowly in several directions, testing the air. No one direction carried more promise than another. But when she walked toward a cluster of bushes near the house she practically stepped on a big, clumsy goose. It plunged away from Emily, neck stretched out, flopping its wings against the air and finally taking off. But the honking continued. Emily startled another goose around the corner of the house. It slapped its feet against the cold sidewalk and eventually pushed itself into the air. Still, the honking continued. It was all around. What was going on?

Emily heard a rustling in the bushes near her cabin and looked there. A goose was flopping its wings on the ground, but without the clumsy energy of the other geese. It was trying to get away from Emily, but couldn't. Something was wrong.

Emily walked behind it. The goose still tried to escape by beating its wings against the ground but remained flightless. The goose honked weakly. In response, the other geese honked back louder and more insistently. The goose lifted itself off the ground, but just barely. Emily figured it must be sick or injured and unable to fly. The other geese must be its flock.

The goose was beating away the last of its energy, trying to escape from Emily. What could she do? Emily stood there, frozen with indecision. She couldn't bear to chase the goose and see it struggle. But she couldn't bear to leave it!

Emily pulled her cabin key from the string around her neck and unlocked her door. She yanked at the bedspread that covered her window and ran outside. Emily opened the blanket wide, pinching the edges in her hand. She was sweating.

The goose, herded by Emily, wobbled feebly, then fell to the ground, spent. Its wings hung open, its neck fell forward. It hadn't enough energy left to gather itself together. Emily scooped it up in the blanket, one arm under the back of its body, one arm under the neck. The goose honked from somewhere deep inside itself. Its voice was muffled and far away. Emily knew the goose must be frightened to be so near a human. But there was no more fight left in it, only still-ness. The heavy warmth of the animal surprised Emily and pleased her.

The goose was becoming heavy in Emily's arms. Emily sat down next to a large tree, and held the goose closer to her chest. She sat there for a long time. Suddenly she realized she didn't have the slightest idea what to do next. She'd never taken care of a goose—she'd never even taken care of a parakeet! And this wild thing depended on her now! She would do anything to make sure the goose survived. She pressed her cheek against the goose's wing. She thought that probably you could feed an animal something so wrong it could die. But water! All animals need water.

"Are you thirsty, fella?" Emily spoke softly so she wouldn't startle the bird. Her voice, alone in the dark, sounded fuzzy and, she thought, com-forting. Emily raised herself slowly, sliding against the back of the tree to balance the weight of the bird.

"I'm going to put you in this old kennel behind my cabin." Emily walked very slowly toward the chicken-wire enclosure. She kicked open the latch with her foot, carefully balancing the goose so it would not be jostled—then she crouched down with the goose and slid inside.

"Here, guy." Emily crouched next to the doghouse. "This is where you're going to stay for a while." Emily slowly unwound the blanket and let it fall open. The light on the parking lot shone on the goose. Good! There didn't seem to be a wound, not a large one anyway. Emily lingered for a few minutes, prolonging the time before she had to put the goose down. She liked the feeling of holding something warm and alive in her arms. Finally, she lowered the goose to the cement floor of the kennel.

"I'll be back in a flash," she promised.

Emily ran to the kitchen. There was a light on but Mother wasn't there. Emily wished Mother had been there. It would have been nice to tell her about the goose. Emily pulled a heavy baking pan out of the cupboard. She filled it with water. The water sloshed against the sides as she walked toward the door, slopping onto the floor.

She placed the water dish beneath the goose's beak. "Are you thirsty, fella?" she crooned. The goose did not move. "Come on," she said, splashing a finger in the water to tempt him. She remembered, then, how Mother used to try to get Emily to eat. She used to scrape together a small pile on the side of Emily's plate and say Emily could have dessert if she ate that much. Mother would beg and threaten and sweet-talk Emily, but nothing worked. Emily just ate what she wanted . . . whenever she was ready. So Emily stopped trying to coax the goose and left to find some food.

Emily walked back to the kitchen for another pan. She tore up some bread and put the pieces inside the pan. There was a lamp on in the living room. Kyle Joseph was reading a news magazine.

"Kyle," Emily said, "do you know anything about geese?"

"A little."

"Do you know what they eat?"

"Well . . ." Kyle closed his magazine and sat up straighter. His shirt collar was open. Emily could see little tufts of hair on his chest. "Water plants, mostly, and bugs. Also corn and other grains."

"Do they eat seed? Birdseed?"

"Well, yes, I'm sure they love birdseed."

There was a bird feeder on the front porch! Inside was birdseed and cracked corn. "Thanks!" Emily called over her shoulder. She yanked the front door open. It banged against the wall as

41

she ran toward the bird feeder. As Emily poured the birdseed into the pan, she heard Kyle close the door softly behind her. He was probably watching her from the window now, wondering what stupid thing she was up to. Emily became conscious of every movement. She put the cover back on the feeder and began walking away. She swung her hips a little and she looked at the birdseed intently, as if it contained the secrets of the universe. Emily's cheeks burned. She paused at the corner of the house to cool off. Her heart was pounding.

"Goose!" Emily called as she approached the kennel. Goose. That sounded dumb. He should have a decent name, for Pete's sake.

She tried a few.

"Gilligan." Too cute.

"Kyle." What if Kyle found out Emily named a goose after him? Die!

"Bruno." Bruno. The only Bruno Emily knew was Bruno Matsdorf, Daddy's poker buddy. He had a mustache and smoked a cigar. He was very big and had bushy eyebrows that stuck out all over. He had a big laugh.

Emily tested the name with her tongue. "Bruno." It seemed right. Emily kicked the latch open and crawled inside the kennel.

Bruno was right where she had left him, next to the doghouse. "This will be a real treat for you, Bruno. Birdseed." Emily shook the pan gently. Bruno cocked his head slightly, eyeing the seed. Emily thought maybe he could smell it. Anyway, he seemed interested and that was a good sign.

"Here's what I'm going to do, Bruno, old buddy." Emily put down the birdseed. "I'm going to leave now and go to my cabin. But I'll be back in the morning with breakfast." Emily looked at Bruno longingly. She wanted to pet him, but she thought it would probably frighten him. So she backed out of the kennel and latched the door behind her. Then she crouched down, clutching the edges of the hexagonal wire shapes with her fingertips, curving them inside. She concentrated on sending healing mental vibrations to the goose. She'd read about that once. What the heck? It might work. Bruno needed all the help he could get.

CHAPTER FOUR

Two Pieces of a Picture

Sunday, for the first time since Daddy had died, Emily woke up easily. She slipped Daddy's Saturday shirt over her head and hung it on the doorknob while she made her bed. Then she folded it carefully and placed it on top of her pillow.

Emily opened her notebook to the day's entry and studied it while she got dressed. She'd made a list in her notebook the night before:

Sunday
1. *Check Bruno.*
2. *Feed/water.*
3. *Change Bruno's bedding?*
4. *Investigate second box in attic.*
5. *Keep an eye on guests.*

44

Emily had never had five things on her list before without having to add something like "get dressed" to it.

She added "get dressed" anyway—and checked it off—because six was such a satisfying number.

Emily snagged her motorcycle jacket and ran through the door, plunging her arms into the sleeves as she went. Outside, it was cold and damp. For the third day in a row it looked like it was going to snow. Emily zipped up her jacket. She hoped Bruno was warm enough.

Emily listened for Bruno's flock, but the yard and the field next door were silent. She walked slowly along the side of the cottage, aware of every twig and dry leaf and the sound they made when she stepped on them. She didn't want to startle Bruno. But it was difficult to be so careful. Emily wanted to run to the kennel. She wanted to make sure Bruno was all right.

Bruno was standing, his long neck stiff and erect. His head swiveled about as he looked over his beak at the morning. Bruno had eaten all his food and drunk his water. He was okay!

Emily was so proud! She wanted to throw her arms around Bruno and squeeze him. She wanted to yell something. She wanted to yell, "*Bruno was hurt and now he's okay and I, Emily, did it!*" She wanted Bruno to grow sleek and fat. She wanted him to waddle behind her wherever she went and lay his long neck on her shoulder when she was lonely.

Bruno shifted his weight and fell heavily from one rubbery black foot to the other. Emily panicked for one horrible moment, thinking he was wounded. But this, she realized with a laugh, was the way he walked. It was absolutely incredible! In order to walk Bruno had to hunch up his heavy rear end like a lady gathering her skirts. Then he swayed back and forth, weaving his neck in the opposite direction. He looked so clumsy!

Sometimes Emily felt clumsy too, like her legs had grown too fast and were too big for her body. Moving them took the biggest effort and mental control. But Bruno—well, this was hysterical! He didn't have a shred of dignity left when he walked.

For months, Emily had felt there wasn't a God. But maybe there was. Maybe God was Someone with a really good sense of humor and the goose was one of His cleverest jokes.

Emily grabbed at her stomach and fell to the ground, laughing. *Bruno looked like Sara Mueller!* He really did! Emily could see Bruno very well, clutching a pink quilted robe to his bosom. He didn't even have to stick a towel in his pants. In fact, he looked like he already had one there.

Oh, this was too much!

Emily pulled herself together and went to the storage shed for more seed. There was a plastic milk carton in the seed bag. Its top was cut off to make a scoop. Emily filled it with seed. The bag was almost empty. How was she going to get more seed unless she told Mother about Bruno? Emily carried the seed to Bruno's cage. When she approached, he edged away from her. Emily lowered herself slowly and slid the seed into Bruno's dish. Then she picked up the water dish and slowly carried it outside with her.

Bruno waddled immediately to his breakfast and started wolfing it down. Seed flew all over, like snow in a blizzard. Bruno was a slob.

Emily went to the kitchen to fill the water dish. Mother was there, mixing batter for pancakes with a big wooden spoon. She was wearing her "uniform," this time her usual lumpy corduroys with a red cotton turtleneck. Her cheeks were flushed. A wisp of hair hung over her eyes. Mother swept it up with the back of her hand, but it soon slid down again. Emily lingered in the doorway. Yesterday she had wanted to tell Mother about the goose. This morning she had wanted to tell the world. But now . . . Well, she wanted to keep it to herself. It made Bruno hers in a way he wouldn't be if she discussed him with someone else.

"Good morning, Mother." Emily looked down at the floor. She felt exuberant, excited. If Mother saw her like that, sparkly, she'd wonder what was up.

"Did you sleep well, dear?"

"Yes," Emily said.

"I thought maybe you had trouble sleeping, with all that noise outside."

"What do you mean?"

"The geese. Didn't you hear them? It sounded like a whole flock right in our yard. They didn't quiet down until two or three."

"Did you hear them this morning?"

"No. . . . Really, I don't know about you young people." Mother poured buttermilk in the batter. "You sleep through anything. Me, I have trouble sleeping every night."

Emily knew it was true. Mother tossed terribly every night. She'd often heard her, even before Daddy died.

Mother blew a jet of air at the hair hanging in her eyes. "I just wish I could forget my troubles when I sleep. But I think about all the things I have to do and I can't relax."

"I'll rub your back some night."

Mother turned around. Her eyes were wide and her eyebrows had arched high into her forehead. "Why, Emily!"

Emily smiled, not a broad smile, but small, elfin.

"I . . . I . . . I . . ." began Mother.

It was great when Mother stuttered!

"That would be . . . very nice."

Mother jerked around and busied herself mixing the pancake batter furiously. Emily knew pancake batter was supposed to be mixed gently, lightly. This stuff was going to be tough as shoe leather. Emily enjoyed seeing Mother embarrassed. She rarely caught her off guard, and when Mother was flustered she seemed more human. Emily might even enjoy giving her a back rub. But now she had to fill Bruno's water dish.

"I'm doing a science project," Emily lied. "And I need some water."

"Help yourself, dear. I'm glad to see you involved in school things."

Emily carried the water dish to the big metal sink, washed out the sticky birdseed, and filled it with fresh water.

In the dining room, Mrs. Sharples was saying, "Isn't it just terrible about Tom Crockett?" Mrs. Sharples shook her head woefully. "He was the late husband of our Agnes, a fairly successful account executive for an advertising agency in Chicago. Well, the man didn't even take out life insurance! Can you imagine such irresponsibility? He died in a tragic motorcycle accident—" Mrs. Sharples leaned over the table and whispered, "He wasn't even wearing a helmet! His death left sweet Agnes with a pile of debts and no way to pay them. That's how she came to run this inn." Mrs. Sharples nodded sharply. "It was her family home, left to her by her parents."

Emily walked through the big swinging door with Bruno's water. "Little pitchers have big ears," Mrs. Sharples said, nodding at Emily pointedly.

Emily glanced at the guests waiting for Mother's pancakes. They were all strangely quiet.

"Ernie," blared Mrs. Sharples, sounding like a foghorn, "you forgot to bring down my pocketbook. Run along and get it for me, won't you, dear?"

Ernie—the mouse!—ran along as ordered.

Mrs. Sharples surveyed the room like a queen, finally focusing on lowly Emily. "Here's that little charmer," she gushed in a voice that dripped syrup. What a fake! Emily ignored her.

"Hello, dear," said Sara Mueller.

Emily almost dropped the water dish. Sara Mueller was sitting ramrod straight. Her head was small compared to her body and she had a long, cone-shaped nose that looked amazingly like a goose's beak. And when Ms. Mueller sat down she settled herself on her big rear end the way a goose settles into its feathers! Emily would never be able to look at Ms. Mueller without seeing her as a goose!

"Hello, Emily," Sara Mueller said again.

Emily didn't look up. She couldn't. "Good morning, Ms. Mueller," she said, gulping down a laugh.

Emily walked quickly to the door, taking small, even steps so she wouldn't spill the water. She heard Ms. Mueller say, "Emily certainly is a hard-working young person. It looks like she's carrying water for livestock."

Sara Mueller was a dope, but she was okay. Emily walked through Mother's room.

"Really, Sara, you're so naive. Emily is a juvenile delinquent. The ungrateful child is nothing but a burden to her poor mother."

Creep! Emily let the outside door slam behind her. She *wouldn't* let Mrs. Sharples bother her.

Emily put Bruno's water dish down on the cement kennel floor. It was getting gross in there, full of gigantic goose droppings. The big, white splodges were all over the place! Emily figured what went in Bruno and what came out must be about the same amount. It was a miracle he got any food value at all. Emily looked inside the doghouse. It was full of droppings, too. Emily went to the north side of the house, where Mother had piled bales of straw against the foundation for insulation. She pulled on a string and dragged a bale back to Bruno's cage. She spread some loose straw in the doghouse and scattered some on the floor of the kennel. There. That was better. Emily settled herself against the door end of the kennel. Bruno was busy on the other end. It was a good idea to hang around in the kennel with him so he could get used to her.

"Bruno," Emily said out loud. It felt funny to talk to Bruno out loud. The truth was, Emily didn't do much talking to anybody these days, and before Bruno, she'd never talked to an animal. But who would know? And it was a good idea for Bruno to get used to Emily's voice.

"Bruno, old pal, I'm afraid I haven't seen your flock around today."

Bruno honked. He hadn't, either.

"Where do you think they are?"

Honk. Gone.

"They wouldn't have left you, would they?"

Honk. Yes.

"Bruno!" Emily reached out toward Bruno, but the movement startled him and he jerked backward. "No, Bruno, I'm sure they're not gone. I bet they're around here someplace, maybe eating in a cornfield or something. They're probably hungry."

Bruno began pacing on the doghouse end of the kennel, mumbling to himself. *Huhnga, huhnga, huhnga.*

"I know what you mean. It's cruel to be left alone, left to *handle* things for yourself. Bruno, don't give up. And Bruno—at least you have me."

"And me." A deep voice echoed behind her. For a minute Emily thought Bruno had spoken but then the awful, humiliating truth dawned on her. It was Kyle and he had heard her talking to Bruno! Emily's cheeks flamed bright red. Despite the icy day she was sweating beneath her jacket.

What could be worse? And she couldn't even run and hide! She was trapped like an animal in a cage!

Kyle walked around to the side of the kennel. "Look at this guy," he said. At least he was focusing attention on the goose instead of Emily. Emily's face began to cool. "Emily, how did you catch him?"

"He was hurt. He couldn't fly. I caught him with a blanket." Emily was a brilliant conversationalist. A real rocket scientist.

"He's a young goose—see how his colors are muddy? Sometimes the young ones get so exhausted they can't fly anymore. The flock will urge them on, if they can. If not, well, the young goose is left behind. Many of them die. But you probably already knew that."

"I didn't."

"Emily, you probably saved his life."

Emily wanted to ask Kyle if he thought the flock was around someplace, but she didn't want to ask in front of Bruno. She wasn't stupid enough to think a bird could understand people. But it had seemed as though Bruno had been talking to her a few minutes ago. Emily had heard that animals often have a strong ESP sense, that they see pictures—images—when people are talking. So she didn't want to discuss Bruno's possible abandonment in front of him.

"Emily, would you mind terribly if I help you with Bruno? Frankly, I'm a little bored here."

"Yeah, I know what you mean. This isn't exactly a swinging crowd, is it?"

Kyle laughed easily. Emily shivered. Kyle's laugh was so tender and natural that it seemed to surround her like an embrace. Emily pictured herself in Kyle's arms. She hoped Kyle didn't have ESP.

"No, it's not a swinging crowd, but I don't go in for that much either. I don't know. I'm just restless. Anyway, the offer still stands. How can I help?"

"I need some seed. There isn't much in the shed. If you wait a sec I'll run in and get some money."

"It's my treat, Emily. I'll take you to the—where do you get seed around here, anyway?"

"The feed mill."

"I'll take you to the feed mill and we can buy a bag of birdseed. Later, maybe I'll spring for a sundae."

And he did. A hot-fudge sundae. Kyle even

paid extra for the toasted pecans. When Emily got back she made the terrible mistake of walking through the living room.

"Somebody's got a boyfriend!" That witch, Mrs. Sharples! Emily kept on walking.

"I remember when I was your age. I had a schoolgirl crush on my eighth-grade teacher. Yes, young lady, these are the best years of your life. I remember . . ."

Emily let the front door slam behind her, slicing Mrs. Sharples' sentence in half. If these were her best years, Emily hated to think what the worst years would be like. Outside, she threw her notebook on the ground and plopped down beside it. She pulled a pencil out of her pocket and wrote: *Expose* Mrs. Sharples *as a jerk!*

Emily underlined Mrs. Sharples so heavily she broke the tip of her pencil. She felt, along with everything else, that Mrs. Sharples was responsible for her broken pencil, too.

What could be more satisfying than exposing Mrs. Sharples' true, disgusting self? Emily thought about it with delicious anticipation. First, she'd have to uncover something to embarrass her with. The ski charade was a sure bet. But Mrs. Sharples was a real witch. Emily needed something bigger than that. And with a little snooping, maybe she could find something really juicy. The place to start was the Sharpleses' room. Emily had snooped in guests' rooms many times before and was, she had to admit, very discreet. She could slip in and out within five minutes. In five minutes she could examine the contents of the wardrobe, suitcase, bedside table, and coat pockets. She left everything exactly as she found it, so no one was ever the wiser.

The key was in planning. You had to have an idea of what you'd be looking for and where you might find it. At the same time, a good investigator kept her eye out for anything unusual. There was a good chance Emily would be a private investigator when she was older, and she thought of this as part of her professional training. And Emily felt that it was her civic duty to expose Mrs. Sharples. Who knew how many people she had already hurt and embarrassed in her lifetime? It would serve her right to see what it felt like. And poor Ernie! He acted like he was on a leash, the way she jerked him around. That was another reason to expose Mrs. Sharples. It would boost Ernie's morale.

Emily was becoming painfully aware of how hard and cold the November ground was. Her butt was freezing! She stood up and walked to the end of the driveway, rubbing her backside with a mittened hand. Well, it was time to check out the attic.

As Emily climbed the second flight, she began to feel a warm glow, a calm, settling over her. She couldn't explain why. She only knew that it felt good and that she was looking forward to exploring the attic.

Emily opened the attic door and groped her way to the light bulb string. She pulled it. Pulling the string gave Emily the weirdest sensation. It was like she "turned on" the room. Maybe there *was* no room until she pulled the string. Maybe it appeared—and actually *formed* when the light turned on.

Which box should she open today? There were so many and a lot of them were probably full of dumb things. She wanted today's box to be a good one, not full of bedsheets. Well, if she got a sheets box she'd open another. After all, opening one box a day was her rule anyway. She could break it if she wanted to. Emily closed her eyes and spun around four times. Then she walked forward, eyes still shut, feeling with her foot until it bumped into something. She opened her eyes and looked down at the box. The box was closed with several wide strips of masking tape. Emily pulled them off easily. Then she unfolded the flaps and looked inside.

Toys! Old toys! Emily pulled out a doll first. It was a hard doll with red hair and blue eyes. She had silvery beads around her neck and a net ballet skirt and satin bodice. She had on real nylons, white ones, with red satin ballet slippers. She was beautiful! Everything was in perfect condition but Emily could tell this doll had been played with a lot. It wasn't pinkish-plasticky, the way a new doll is, but had a dull glow to it that comes from handling something carefully and often. Emily bent the doll's legs and sat her on an old couch pillow so she could watch Emily. The doll had eyes that could close, and Emily figured her eyes had been closed long enough. She would probably enjoy watching things for a while.

Then Emily pulled out a dog, grayish blue with droopy ears. It had been squeezed so much the stuffing was condensed. That left the dog limp and wobbly. It was kind of nice that way because it formed to Emily's body so perfectly. Emily slumped it on her shoulder. The dog's legs hung down on each side. Emily liked the feel of it there so she left it while she continued to explore.

Books. A bunch of them, thirty or more. They were all hardcover books, most with their paper covers still on. Emily figured they were pretty old, and wondered whether there was such a thing as paperback books back then, *whenever back then was.* The books had been placed in the box spine side up so Emily could read the titles easily.

Little House on the Prairie. Treasure Island. Eloise. The Travels of Sacajawea. Proper Etiquette for the Young Girl—this looked practically brand-new.

These were children's books, probably a girl's. Emily dropped *Proper Etiquette for the Young Girl* right on her foot when she thought: Mother's!

These were Mother's books, Mother's doll, and stuffed dog! Emily could hardly imagine Mother playing with a stuffed dog. She figured Mother's toys—if she'd had any—would have been little kitcheny things like a tiny oven that really worked and a little ironing board and iron.

This put a whole new light on Mother, but still, Emily couldn't make things fit together. It was as if she had two pieces of a picture that had been ripped in half. But when she put the pieces side by side they were from different photographs. The Mother Emily knew was stiff, hardworking, joyless, someone who would have read *Proper Etiquette for the Young Girl.* It couldn't be the same person who played with a ballerina doll and a stuffed dog!

The second level of books revealed a real treas-ure. *Game Birds of North America.* A Canada goose was a game bird and this was North America, so Emily was pretty sure it would have something about Bruno. She picked up the book. It was deep red, almost brown, and smelled like an old li-brary. The long outside edges of the pages were soft and fuzzy, especially in the middle. Mother must have read this book a lot. Emily scanned the index, looking for a promising chapter. There it was. The Canada goose (pages 87–95). Emily could read the chapter tonight. Emily wrote:

Item 2—Doll, stuffed dog. Books. Game Birds of North America, *very used.* Proper Etiquette for the Young Girl, *like new.*

Emily put the rest of the books back in the box. It made her feel cozy to think about the end of today. She'd sit in bed, wearing Daddy's Satur-day shirt, and eat something. Popcorn. She'd make out her list of things to do tomorrow after school and then she'd read about the Canada goose.

CHAPTER FIVE

Beth Returns

November was a funny month. The cold smacked Emily silly. She kept thinking, "Is this what winter is like?" It wasn't as if she'd never been through winter before, because Chicago gets cold, too. But in Chicago there are things to do and places to go. Light and heat and people pour out of apartments onto the streets so it doesn't feel so cold and dark. But there wasn't a single apartment in Ellison Bay, and most of the shops closed after tourist season. Door County is a peninsula, but there's a channel of water that separates it from the rest of Wisconsin. You have to cross a bridge to get there. The tourists leave after Labor Day, mostly for Chicago. The natives say they roll up the bridge then, because after that, they're on their own. And it gets dark so early in November.

Emily hadn't heard Bruno's flock since that first night. Now it was Monday, after school, and she still hadn't seen them. It was entirely possible, however, that they were still around, just waiting quietly. The first place Emily looked was in the shrubbery around the house. It didn't seem likely that the flock would be there. But you never knew. She whistled and clapped her hands. If any geese were hiding she wanted to startle them into flight.

The flock was not in the yard. Next, Emily searched the cornfield. She had to walk back and forth in the rows between the cornstalks, so it took a long time. Her hands were red and numb and she wished she'd worn mittens. The flock was not in the cornfield. Emily walked through two more fields. She walked up and down the road in front of the house and she even walked to the lake. No geese.

It was nearly evening when Emily got back to the storage shed and scooped up more seed for Bruno. Slowly, she carried it to his cage. "Here, Bruno," she called. "I'm bringing food and water." As Emily got closer, Bruno backed into the corner. He didn't trust her yet. But he would. Maybe tomorrow.

Emily slid the seed into Bruno's dish. She crawled back and waited a few minutes to see if he'd warm up to her. But Bruno remained frozen, eyeing her nervously, his head cocked slightly to the side.

Now. She had to tell him now. "Bruno, I searched all over for your flock. I looked through the cornfield, two other fields, down the road, and the lake. Bruno, your flock was not there. They've gone."

Hoonk. Emily thought Bruno's honk wavered a little.

"Bruno, it's true. They really have gone."

Honk!

"I know. Believe me, I know. Your mother and father were probably in the flock . . . and your friends. They left you! How *could* they? It's like they didn't love you enough to stick around. Things get tough and off they go."

Hooooooonk. Hoooooonk. Hoooonk.

"That's right, fella. You'll feel better after a good cry." Emily moved toward the big goose. She inched so slowly that she did not frighten him away. All the while she was picturing comforting things: warm feathers, a nest, the moon at night, a gentle lake. "Bruno, I will stay with you *forever.* I'll never leave you and I'll always

64

take care of you. You can count on me, Bruno."

Emily remained in the kennel for a long time even though she was very cold and it was hard to sit still for so long. She wanted Bruno to know how faithful she was. As she turned to go she saw Mother.

"Emily, what is this?"

"A goose, Mother. A Canada goose."

"I know what a goose is, Emily. I meant what is it doing here?"

"He was too tired to fly with the flock. They left him behind."

"Don't I have enough people to take care of without having to care for a goose?" Mother stepped closer to the cage. She was glaring over Emily with her arms folded.

Emily wished she could stand up. She wished she could run. "I'm taking care of Bruno. You don't have to."

"And I suppose you'll buy the seed yourself?"

"Kyle bought some for me."

Mother was silent for a minute. Then she said, "I'll tell you one thing, Emily, under no circumstances am I going to take care of this goose. If you forget, he'll just go hungry."

"Don't worry about it. He won't go hungry." Emily clipped each word short.

Mother continued, "What really hurts me is that you didn't tell me. I had to come out here and find you and the goose. It's like you purposefully cut me out, Emily."

Emily said nothing. She would not give Mother the satisfaction of responding. Emily remembered the times when Mother harped at Daddy. Maybe he let himself die because Mother drove him to it.

After a while Mother left. Emily found that she was shaking. Tears stung at her eyes.

Hoonk.

Emily looked up. "Bruno!" Emily wanted to hold Bruno but she knew he wasn't ready to let her. Anyway, it felt good to have him close. Maybe he was flashing mental images to her. Emily tried to clear her mind so she could see Bruno's images. But she kept picturing Mother glowering down at her.

" 'Bye, Bruno. I'll be back later."

Emily crawled out of the kennel. When she headed for the attic she did so quietly. Under no circumstances did she want Mother to find her in the attic.

Mother was really a jerk to blow up like that. Emily's body stung as if she'd been slapped by Mother's hand instead of her words. Emily hoped she would not find a box that would make her feel sorry for Mother or something. She didn't want to feel anything but anger at Mother right now. Emily shook her head. What the heck! She could look at a box with scientific objectivity. She didn't have to feel anything.

Emily walked decisively to a smallish box. She sliced open the tape with a dinner knife she'd brought along. The first thing she pulled out was a leash, a dog leash. It was brown leather, crackled with age or use, Emily wasn't sure which. There was also a large dog dish. AESOP was printed on the side of the dish. There were also a brush, a choke collar, a whistle, and a handbook on Brittany spaniels. Beneath everything was a large plaid cushion.

So Mother had had a dog. The dog was probably perfectly trained. That's why there was a whistle—it was for calling the dog. Emily played around with the choke collar, trying to figure out how to make it into a circle. Finally she figured out that you had to let the chain fall through one of the large rings at one end. Emily snapped the leash onto the collar and dragged it along the floor of the attic. It would be nice, she thought, to be able to lead around a pet, to have something live tugging at the other end. Maybe she could

train Bruno to follow her on a leash. Emily knew
Mother must have loved Aesop, maybe the way
Emily loved Bruno.

Emily wrote:

Item 3—Dog stuff.

Mother usually ate dinner alone in the kitchen
after the dishes were done. Maybe tonight, Emily
thought, I'll eat with her. But when Emily walked
into the kitchen, she saw that her tray was already stacked with food. She could still say something now, before Mother began serving the
guests. Emily almost said, "I'd rather eat with
you, Mother." In her mind, she could hear herself saying that. She could see Mother light up
with surprise and slowly, tenderly, remove the
food from Emily's tray. But, in fact, Emily remained silent. Why didn't she say something?
Why did she sit there like a lump and not say
something?

Emily picked up one of the dish covers to look
at the food inside.

"We're having salmon loaf, creamed potatoes,
and peas," Mother said as she arranged sprigs
of parsley on one of the serving platters.

"Yuck. I hate salmon loaf." Emily's voice was louder than she wanted it to be.

"Emily!" Mother spooned creamed potatoes into a serving bowl. Her voice was tight and her shoulders were hunched high. "Really, you are so picky!" She swept a jar of peanut butter from the cupboard and spread some on a piece of bread. Then she went to the refrigerator and balanced a bottle of milk, a pitcher of cream, and peach jelly in one arm while she kicked the refrigerator closed with one foot. Mother added jelly to Emily's sandwich. Then she scraped the salmon loaf off Emily's plate and put the sandwich in its place. But the sandwich would smell like fish now, because it was right on top of where the salmon had been.

"Can I have a different plate?"

Silently, swiftly, Mother took a plate from the cupboard. She spun around to put it on Emily's tray when the plate slipped from her hands and crashed to the tile floor. She bent down to pick up the pieces and then stopped. She pressed her fingers to her temples. She was shaking. Her eyes were closed and she was breathing quickly. It frightened Emily to see Mother out of control again. Was she going to burst out crying? Was she going to harp at Emily? Emily didn't want to hang around to find out, so she grabbed her tray with the fishy-smelling sandwich and ran to her room.

Emily ate part of the sandwich. Maybe Bruno would like the rest. Emily tore the sandwich into pieces as she walked toward the kennel. "Hi, Bruno, I'm back." Emily stood outside the kennel and threw the pieces through the wire. Bruno waddled eagerly toward the food. "And for zis evening's dinner, m'sieur, we 'ave Salmon-Peanut-Butter Cutlet d'Emily." Bruno's cone-shaped head plunged forward, dragging the fat, clumsy body behind it. He bolted the smaller pieces down whole and snapped his beak at the larger ones until he'd worked them down to a gulpable size.

"I see, m'sieur, that we approve of ze cutlet." Bruno jerked his neck around frantically, scanning the ground for a piece he might have missed. He paused for a moment to let a white, slimy blob slide from his back end.

"Oh, m'sieur, a tip, I see. Zank you so very much."

Satisfied, finally, that he'd eaten it all, Bruno wriggled to the ground and settled himself into his feathers.

Emily stuck out her own rear end and settled

down to the ground, wriggling the way Bruno had. She extended her neck and swiveled it around, peering at the world from behind her nose. "Hhhonk. Hhhonk."

Bruno jerked his head from side to side, examining Emily more closely.

"Hhhonk."

"Honk!"

Emily choked down a laugh as she raised herself up to a crouch. She folded her arms at her sides like wings and waddled, her rear end hanging out. "Hhhonk Hhhonk."

That's when she noticed the headlights swinging into the parking lot. Usually guests didn't arrive on Monday night. Emily squinted into the headlights. The car was small and red. It was Beth Thomas! She'd come back to Kyle.

"Can I help you with your suitcase?" Emily asked.

Beth laughed. Her laugh was deep and smooth. "Sure, Em." Beth threw an arm over Emily's shoulders and walked with her into the inn. "Do you think your mother has room for me?"

"Sure. I'm sure she does."

Beth rang the bell at the desk and said, "Thanks, Em." She held a dollar toward Emily.

"No, really. Keep it, Miss Thomas."

"Okay. Then I get to treat you to a big pile of Swedish pancakes with lingonberry sauce."

"Deal."

Emily walked away from Beth. She breathed in her perfume until the scent disappeared. Then, when Beth was looking the other way, Emily crouched behind the sofa. She wanted to see the reunion. Probably heavy eye contact, meaningful. A few intimate words. Two bodies, pressed together. Emily didn't want to miss a thing! She pulled out her notebook and pencil and wrote:

Beth Thomas entered the inn wearing fur après ski boots and dove-gray slacks. Subject is also wearing a fur jacket with matching hat. The pile of the fur is deep and luxurious indicating that the subject is very wealthy.

Beth flicked off her hat and ran one hand through her honey-colored hair. It was bluntly cut and silky, and it ran in a smooth line, even with her chin. It had been done, Emily was certain, in an expensive Chicago salon by someone with a foreign-sounding name. Beth was so mature and sophisticated!

Beth spun around the postcard carousel, looking at one card and then another while she waited for Mother to register her. The stairs creaked. Emily did not miss the look on Beth's face as she waited to see who was coming down the stairs.

She wrote *hopeful anticipation* in her notebook without looking at the page. She hoped she'd be able to read it later, but—no matter what!—she was not going to look down and miss watching the love scene.

It was Kyle. "Beth, I thought you had to . . ."

"I changed my mind."

Kyle walked carefully, as if he were walking on delicate Fabergé eggs, and all the while he didn't stop looking at Beth. Beth smiled a wide, eager grin. She brushed her hair behind her ear and Emily noticed for the first time that her face was sprinkled with light freckles.

Mother entered the room then, but Emily was the only one who noticed her. Beth and Kyle whispered, fingers laced, their heads bent together. Mother walked behind the desk. Kyle held Beth's face in both hands and began kissing her tenderly. Mother waited behind the desk. Beth wound her arms around Kyle's neck, still holding her hat in one hand. Mother cleared her throat. Beth's hand slid into Kyle's hair, dropping her hat, holding him closer, more passionately. "You'll be staying a few extra days, Miss Thomas?" Mother enquired politely.

"Miss Thomas" did not respond, at least not to Mother.

"It looks as though that will be the case. I'll just put your name down here and assign you to your old room, Number 4."

Beth and Kyle were still kissing. Emily figured, at this point, their visual traffic pattern was about one centimeter.

"Well, if you'll excuse me now," said Mother, closing the guest register, "I'll get back to the kitchen."

"I thought you had an important meeting," said Kyle.

"I did," said Beth with an impish grin. "But I called Bill Wassermann and said I had large, painful boils all over my face and that, even though my doctor said they were contagious, we could still meet if he was careful not to get too close."

"I see. Of course, Mr. Wassermann couldn't trust himself not to get too close to you."

"I guess not. He said, now that I mentioned it, he'd overlooked something on his own calendar that made our meeting very inconvenient. He wondered if we could reschedule our meeting for—how long would I be contagious?—a week from now." Kyle and Beth laughed. Emily wondered how Beth would look with boils on her face.

Emily put her index and middle fingers together, like lips. Then she pressed them to her own mouth. She wondered what it would feel like to kiss someone passionately. She'd kissed boys before, but they were only quick, embarrassed kisses with cold lips.

When Beth and Kyle walked outside, Emily got out from behind the couch and sat down. She wrote furiously—she wanted to get all the details down while everything was still fresh in her mind.

She wrote:

> *The two lovers, drawn by a relentless force, bent into each other's arms. They kissed tenderly at first, then with quickening force. Kyle's hot, wet lips consumed Beth's and she melted into his arms.*

Emily leaned into the cushions of the couch. It was easy to imagine herself in Kyle's arms instead of Beth. Was it crazy to think Kyle was beginning to like Emily, just a little? Maybe, if Beth hadn't returned, Kyle would have grown to love Emily.

She wrote:

This is stupid. What makes me think any boy could love me, let alone Kyle? There are forty boys in my class. Not one has ever asked to go with me to a dance. No one has promised to meet me at a movie and no one has even slammed my locker. Not that I would want them to. My class has the dumbest collection of hicks I've ever seen and the boys are the worst.

The least-worst boys are: Kevin H., Ryan P., and John P. If one of these boys talked to me I would probably talk back.

"Emily." Emily jerked upright, startled.

Mother was standing there, lumpish. Her hair was straggly and she looked tired and frumpy. Emily was embarrassed for her. Mother looked like a dishrag next to Beth.

"Yes?"

Mother sat down heavily, next to Emily. "I just thought we might talk, dear. We don't have much time together now."

"You're pretty busy."

"Yes, that's true. But I'm never too busy for you. Nothing is more important than you, Emily."

Just great! Mother must have been reading child psychiatry. Now she was going to try to get some "quality time" in with Emily. "What do you want to talk about?"

"Nothing special." Mother slid her wedding ring up and down her finger. "I was just wondering . . . um . . . well, how you're doing in school."

"Fine, Mother."

"Tell me about it."

Emily was right. This was psychiatry talk. "School is just . . . school. Everything is fine, Mother. Really."

"Yes. Well. I'm sure that's true. Have you made any friends?"

"Sure."

"That's good. It's a good thing to have friends."

Which was funny. Mother had no friends.

Mother peeked over the top of Emily's notebook. "What are you writing, dear?"

"Nothing." Emily quickly laid the open notebook against her lap, hiding the inside page from Mother's eyes. But, by hiding the inside page, Emily had exposed the *outside* page. That was the part about how Kyle's hot, wet lips had consumed Beth's. Emily tried not to draw attention to it by looking at it, but the words absolutely screamed off the page. Emily leaned her forearm over the notebook in what she hoped was a casual-looking gesture.

"Is it homework?"

"Yes!" Emily felt the perspiration on her face instantly cool with relief.

"That's good, dear. You should keep up with your assignments and do well in school."

"Right." And then what? Do well in school and get a job and work like a slave for the rest of your life?

Mother patted Emily on the hand. "I'm glad we had this little talk, Emily." Mother went into her room and closed the door.

Emily took a deep breath and let her arm fall slowly from the top of her notebook.

CHAPTER SIX

Behind the Wall

The entry for Tuesday read:

Tuesday

1. *School (yuck!).*
2. *Take care of Bruno.*
3. *Open fourth box in attic.*
4. *Try to get into Mrs. S's room.*

When I'm in school I pretend I'm somewhere else, like performing in a Chicago nightclub or riding through the Rockies on the back of somebody's Harley. I don't ask questions, don't talk to the hicks, and do what I have to and no more.

Tuesday morning, at school, Mike Halper kept hanging around Emily. Mike was Emily's lab partner. He was pretty cute.

79

"So, Emily, are you ready for the exam on Thursday?"

"No," Emily said.

"Me either. I'm really going to have to study to get a good grade."

"Yeah."

"Hey, Emily, do you want to study together after school tonight?"

Emily looked closely at Mike's face. He looked eager, hopeful, like a puppy. "I can't. I have to take the bus home."

"Oh," Mike said sadly. He began to walk away.

Emily stopped him. "Maybe some other time."

"Maybe." Mike turned again.

"Mike, I have a wild Canada goose at home, Bruno. He was too weak to fly and I'm feeding him and letting him rest. Maybe you'd like to come over sometime and see him."

Mike smiled broadly. "Yeah. Maybe," he said, and walked away.

Just before school was dismissed, Emily was called into the counselor's office. She was expecting it.

Mr. Wimer, the counselor, shook Emily's hand and then led her to a chair in his office. He sat down and leaned back in the chair, his hands

80

behind his head. "Emily. We are happy to have you here at Gibraltar School."

"Well, Mr. Wimer," Emily said enthusiastically, "it's my pleasure. You have a fine school here." If there was one thing Emily knew, it was how to talk counselor talk. She'd had many little "chats" with counselors when Daddy died. She knew how to string them along.

Mr. Wimer smiled appreciatively. "Are you happy at Gibraltar?" He meant, "Are you showing signs of depression? Are you on drugs or suicidal?"

"I sure am, Mr. Wimer." Always call a counselor by name. It shows sincerity.

"And, Emily, are you happy at home?" Mr. Wimer asked. He leaned forward in his chair, in order to maintain closer personal contact with Emily.

"Why, yes. Mother and I are just fine."

Mr. Wimer looked puzzled. He apparently questioned Emily's integrity. Maybe she was too enthusiastic. She decided she had to play it down a little.

Emily sat up straight, to show she wasn't depressed or on drugs. "Of course, only time will heal the wound of losing a loved one."

Mr. Wimer nodded sympathetically.

"But on the whole," Emily continued, "I'm adjusting fine to school. Oh, I have little problems here and there—everybody does." Counselors want you to show signs of realism. "But on the whole, I'm quite happy. The truth is, Mr. Wimer, I'm not the brightest student. I try hard, but I've just never gotten what you'd call good grades."

Mr. Wimer said, "Your teachers seem to think you're quite bright. They think you aren't rising to your full potential."

So Emily said, "I'm flattered that they think I'm smart. Maybe I am, Mr. Wimer, maybe I'm just a late bloomer."

"Have you made any friends, Emily?"

He had Emily there. What could she say? "Not yet, Mr. Wimer, but I'm sure I will. These things just take time." Then Emily rose up *briskly* and shook Mr. Wimer's hand. "I really appreciate your confidence in me, Mr. Wimer. I'm going to get on that bus right now and get busy with my homework. Thank you for this talk."

Mr. Wimer stood there with his mouth open. Clearly, the interview had not gone the way he'd intended.

Emily was eager to get off the bus. Bruno was waiting. "You seem chipper this afternoon," Emily said as she walked toward the big bird. Emily noticed a sign just above the kennel, one she hadn't noticed before. The writing was nearly illegible; most of it had weathered down to the wood. But Emily could make it out. It said, "Aesop." This was Aesop's kennel, she thought.

Bruno had been waddling around his cage, plopping his rubbery feet against the wet leaves and cement, clucking to himself. He stopped clucking when he saw Emily and backed up calmly as she entered his cage.

"You know what, Bruno? I think you're getting used to me." Emily slid the scoop of food into Bruno's dish, and crouched on the other side of the cage and watched him wolf down his meal. Emily had grown to depend on Bruno as much as he depended on her. She needed him to be there, waiting. He was something warm and solid who didn't care whether she was rising to her potential or not. Emily thought wistfully of the day he would waddle up to her to greet her! He would honk impatiently when he heard her voice, waiting for her to join him.

"Bruno," Emily began, "there's this kid at school, Mike. He's my lab partner. He keeps trying to talk to me, like he doesn't know everyone thinks I'm stuck up. See, that's what the kids at school say about me, they say I'm stuck up. Well, everybody thinks so, except for Mike, so no one talks to me."

Bruno stopped eating long enough to look at Emily.

"You probably don't know how it is, Bruno. Probably there were no cliques in your flock. Probably everybody was nice to each other. But in school it's different. In school, everybody is *something*. They're a brain or a nerd or a jock or a jerk or a rich kid or—like me—stuck up. Once they have you figured out that's the way you're treated for*ever*. Except for Mike."

Bruno waddled through his food dish, spilling the seed. He stood in his food dish while he drank water. Bruno didn't sip his water. He didn't lap it gently with his tongue. He clapped it with his beak like two hands in the water, splashing all over himself. The spilled seed stuck to his wet feathers. He was not a pretty sight!

"Bruno, you're such a slob!"

"Honk!"

"I know you're not *really* a slob, Bruno. You're used to drinking from a stream or lake or something, not a baking pan. But do you think you can stay clean for a little while? I have other things to do, you know, besides keeping you clean and fed."

Hnonk.

"Good. 'Bye for now." Emily turned quickly and headed for the house. It was almost dark outside now, and she wanted to get to the attic before supper. On the porch, though, she turned around for one last look at the big goose before she headed up to the attic.

"Hello, Emily," whined a voice from the living room. Mrs. Sharples.

Emily paused on the stairs, then continued walking up.

"What do we say, dear?" insisted Mrs. Sharples.

"How do you do, Mrs. Barfles," said Emily, dripping innocent sweetness.

"*Sharp*les, dear. Sharples."

"Oh, yes," said Emily, slapping her forehead. "Sharples. How could I forget?"

"I'm sure I don't know," Mrs. Sharples said.

Emily continued up the stairs. As she swung around to head up the second flight of stairs she saw Mother. Mother was sitting on the steps. Her eyes were closed and her head was in her hands. She looked so thin, sitting there like that. Emily

85

could see the bony outline of her shoulder blades through her turtleneck.

"Mother!"

Mother sucked in a breath quickly and looked up. There were dark rings beneath her eyes and her face was puffy and pale.

"What's wrong?"

"Oh, nothing, Emily. I was just resting here for a minute." Mother raised herself slowly, painfully.

"Are you all right?"

"Oh, yes, I'm fine. Just tired maybe. There's so much work. It never ends."

Mother held the railing and walked slowly downstairs. She stopped and turned. "Thanks for asking, Emily."

Mother was always tired. More now, maybe, than before Daddy died. But still, always tired. It was her own fault. She was the one who insisted that every room be spotless and every meal have homemade rolls and dessert.

"Mrs. Crockett!" Emily heard Mrs. Sharples call from downstairs. She crouched on the stairway to listen. "I just had a little chat with your daughter, and do you know what she called me?"

"No, what?" Mother said.

"She called me Mrs. Barfles. Barfles!"

"Maybe it was a mistake, Mrs. Sharples. Maybe you didn't hear Emily correctly."

"I hardly think so," Mrs. Sharples said. "Well, I just wanted you to know. I'm sure you want to keep the upper hand with that child and you should know what she's up to. You know, if she were my daughter I'd make sure she was kept busy. Perhaps she could do more of the cleaning or baking."

"Perhaps."

"Idle hands are the devil's workshop, you know."

"I wouldn't know."

"No, of course not, dear. You're a very busy person, anyone can see that. And I really don't mean to interfere. It's just that . . . well . . . we don't want that child turning out to be a bad sort, do we?"

"Thank you, Mrs. Sharples," Emily heard Mother say. "I'll keep your advice in mind."

Emily paused before opening the door to the attic. She wanted to savor the excitement, the not knowing. Then she swung the door open and walked into the darkness, her hands reaching out. When the string brushed Emily's arm she pulled it and flooded the attic with light. The attic had become familiar to Emily. It felt like a friend waiting to share a secret. Emily closed her eyes and spun around several times, walking slowly forward, testing the air with her foot. When it bumped into something she opened her eyes.

A sled! Emily bent down to look at it. It had a wooden top with red metal runners. FLEXIBLE FLYER was printed on top. Emily had gotten a sled like it for Christmas one year. She'd never used it much, not in Chicago. When Emily turned the sled over, she saw that there was some writing on it. The writing had been burned on with a wood-burning pen. It was uneven, probably made by a child. Emily had to look closely to read it. It said, "This is the property of Agnes Thorgeson."

Emily ran her finger along the letters. It was a funny feeling to know that Mother had printed the letters. Emily tried to picture Mother on the sled, racing down a hill, but couldn't. Emily had always figured Mother was . . . Mother! Basically the same, just miniature. The thought of a tiny little Mother wearing lumpy corduroys and turtlenecks, with a timer clipped to her little waist, struck Emily as hysterical. She just couldn't picture Mother on a sled. Yet she must have used it, because it had lots of scratches and gouges.

It would be interesting, Emily thought, to see what Mother would say if she saw this sled. Emily decided to take it downstairs. She'd observe Mother's reaction and write it in her notebook.

Emily carried the sled to the attic door and propped it against a wall. She decided that the sled didn't count as a box, so she walked to the middle of the room, closed her eyes, and spun around. Eyes still closed, Emily walked forward, reaching out with her hand and tapping the air with her foot. She walked right into a wall! Emily opened her eyes. She stared at the wall in front of her for several seconds before she realized there was something peculiar about it. Part of the wall—probably where her hand struck it—was caved in. A one-foot-by-one-foot square had been carefully cut into the plywood side and was now caved in. Emily grabbed the square with her fingertips and carefully wriggled it out. There were a lot of things inside, tiny things, but it was too dark to see.

Emily ran out of the attic, down the stairs to the second-floor hallway. There was a flashlight in the table drawer, used for times the inn was without electricity. As Emily reached for the flashlight she saw Mrs. Sharples walk past, smiling smugly. Emily grabbed the flashlight and leaped up the stairs again, two at a time. She shone the flashlight inside the wall opening.

Emily could hardly believe it! Inside was a miniature, three-dimensional fantasy world! There was a blue stream running down the middle of the scene. It was cut out of paper and covered with plastic wrap with blue sequins underneath. The plastic and sequins made it look like real water. Floating in the stream was a paper leaf that was curled up at the sides. A clay bug (a grasshopper?) was tucked inside. He was paddling the leaf like a canoe! A red-and-white checkered cloth was spread on one of the hills. There was a tiny paper picnic basket with chicken legs, watermelon, and pie inside. A family of ladybugs was eating the feast. One of the ladybugs had spilled his drink on the cloth and there was a dark spot underneath his overturned glass. Geese suspended by threads flew overhead.

In the far corner of the scene was a tree with a tree house built on top. Two caterpillars made of pipe cleaners inhabited the tree house. Inside was a small hammock, a milkweed pod, a matchbox television, and a felt butterfly costume you could slip over the caterpillar's body. There was a tube (a straw) slide for an exit. Emily touched the tiny caterpillars with a finger. She thought about how much fun it would be to live in a caterpillar tree house.

Emily found herself thinking of things she could add to the fantasy. She could make bushes out of wire and crepe paper. She could make a little bird's nest and carve a bird jazz combo to put inside. Instruments could be made of nutshells and twigs!

Emily wrote in her notebook:

Items 4 and 5—Sled, Flexible Flyer. Fantasy World.
The Fantasy World was created by someone who was creative, patient, and full of fun. The only logical subject is Mother, though her current personality seems completely unlike her personality as a child. If this is true (and it has to be!), then what made Mother change?

Emily turned out the light and carried the sled downstairs. She leaned it against the wall in the dining room. Then she went to the living room and hunkered down in a sofa. Soon she heard Sara Mueller's gentle voice. "Agnes, would you mind terribly if I help you in the kitchen?"

"No, really, you've done so much already," objected Mother feebly.

"Don't be silly. Let's go." Emily carried the notebook to the dining room table. She could hear Mother and Ms. Mueller perfectly from here.

"What's first?" Ms. Mueller asked.

"A chocolate torte."

"It's awfully late to be starting a torte, Agnes. I have a recipe for apple crisp that is both delicious and quick. Will you let me make that?"

"That would be very nice."

Emily heard the banging of pans in the kitchen. Then, "Have you ever tried instant mashed potatoes, Agnes?"

"No, I haven't."

"They're not bad. I can hardly tell the difference. Why don't you try them?"

"I couldn't do that—the guests expect home-cooked meals."

"Rubbish! We're all just delighted to have such a lovely place to stay and a meal put in front of us. You work so hard, Agnes, but there's just so much you can do. You're entitled to take some shortcuts. I'll tell you what. You make a bowl of homemade mashed potatoes. I'll run to the store while my apple crisp is baking and bring back a package of instant potatoes. We'll make a bowl of those, too, then we'll see if anyone notices the difference."

Before long, Emily saw Sara Mueller walk out of the kitchen, apparently to get the instant potatoes. Soon Mother bolted out the kitchen door. She called to Ms. Mueller. Ms. Mueller turned. "Yes?"

"Sara, could you pick up a fashion magazine for me, a can of cocoa, and some miniature marshmallows?"

"Sure, Agnes," she said, and left.

Then Mother turned and saw the sled. She approached it gently, and slowly ran a finger down one of the runners. She grabbed a corner of her apron and brought it to her eyes. Mother was crying!

CHAPTER SEVEN

From the Bottom of the Well

Every day for a whole week had held the promise of snow. The clouds were heavy, dark, and low. The world seemed poised, as if waiting for the explosion of flakes, able to do nothing else in the meantime. Emily was tired of it. Emily was tired of waiting for Mrs. Sharples, too. She kept watching for a chance to explore her room, but the old busybody had eyes in the back of her head! She hardly left her room and never left the inn. How could Emily snoop under conditions like that?

And Emily was tired of Mother. She looked so worn out and droopy that it was depressing just to look at her. Couldn't she fix herself up or something? Emily found herself thinking about the young-Mother, the girl in the attic. Was it possible that the young-Mother was still inside her? And the biggest mystery still remained: What made Mother change in the first place?

Thursday

1. *Get assigned new lab partners at school.*
2. *Take care of Bruno.*
3. GET IN MRS. S'S ROOM!!!
4. *Let hair grow out to look like Beth's.*
5. *Discover 6th item in attic.*

We switched lab partners today. I got Theresa G. Theresa has a lot of b.o. and I considered sending her a pamphlet anonymously that explains the importance of daily hygiene in the adolescent. But it probably wouldn't do any good anyway and it might hurt her feelings. I know that sometimes I hurt people's feelings. I don't know why I do that. I don't want to.

If it hadn't been for Bruno and the boxes in the attic, Emily would probably have gone crazy. Over the past few days she had discovered a box of Mor's lingerie (including some positively hysterical corsets. Emily tried one on. It felt like she was being squeezed by a boa constrictor!) and a box of bookkeeping records from Far's shipping business.

Emily climbed the stairs now to see if Mrs. Sharples was in her room.

"Ernie, if I've told you once I've told you a thousand times to put the suitcase on the right-hand side of the bed. If I get up in the middle of the night and . . ."

She was in. Darn it! Emily was really in the mood to do some detective work. Well, maybe she'd walk down the hall to see who was in. Mr. Ganopolis had left, so Room 7 was empty. Mr. Fredrich, a new guest, was in Room 6. Emily listened at the door. Not a sound. But she couldn't think of a thing worth discovering in Mr. Fredrich's room, so she moved on. Emily paused outside Room 8. Nothing. She put her ear up to the door. Nothing. She knocked softly. No answer. Quickly, silently, Emily drew the key from her waist and opened up Kyle's room. She closed the door behind her.

The room smelled faintly of men's cologne, something expensive and outdoorsy. Emily opened the pine wardrobe. The scent was a little stronger in there. Emily straightened a slightly crooked sport jacket on its hanger and brushed a piece of lint off the sleeve. She breathed in deeply, filling her lungs with the woodsy scent before gently closing the wardrobe door. She hadn't gone through any of the pockets of Kyle's clothes. She didn't want to.

Emily walked over to Kyle's bedside table. She picked up his alarm clock, which was set for six A.M. Kyle always got up early. He was a jogger. Emily was glad he kept in shape. Emily set the clock down gently. She picked up his wooden hairbrush and ran her finger down the length of it.

". . . be ready in a minute."

It was Kyle! Emily dove under the bed.

She heard Beth laugh softly outside of the door. "Don't take too long." Her voice sounded like water in a stream.

"I won't." Kyle was practically whispering.

"Promise?"

"Promise." Then nothing. Probably they were kissing. After a while she heard the key slide into the lock. Emily felt a small rush of air as Kyle opened the door. Her heart was pounding. She squeezed her eyes shut. "Please don't look under the bed!" she prayed. "Please, please, please, please!"

After a while, she opened her eyes. Kyle had taken off his shoes and socks. His feet were so close to the bed that Emily could easily have touched them. The wrinkle marks from his socks were pressed into Kyle's bare feet. Emily hoped his shoes weren't too tight. Kyle should wear comfortable shoes.

Suddenly, Emily felt the bottom of the mattress press in on her as Kyle sat on the bed. She flattened herself to the floor, making her body as thin and small as she could. She hoped Kyle couldn't hear her breathing!

The bed creaked again and Emily saw Kyle's feet, now in some hiking boots. Then she saw his hands appear and reach for the untied shoelaces. His hands were large and strong-looking. The veins bulged out. What if he bends down far enough to see me? Emily thought.

But he didn't. Kyle got off of the bed, walked toward the door, and opened it. He was leaving! Emily was safe!

"Why, Mr. Joseph!" came Mother's voice from the hall. "I was just about to clean your room. Do you mind?"

"Of course not, Mrs. Crockett. Take your time. I'll be out for an hour or so."

"Fine," said Mother. "Enjoy yourself!" Then Mother walked in. She rolled a vacuum cleaner in front of her. She bent over to plug it in and began vacuuming the carpet next to Kyle's bed. Then she vacuumed underneath.

Emily had to dart and dodge to stay away from the vacuum cleaner, which Mother kept jabbing underneath the bed. It wasn't really that hard to keep out of the way, though, because Mother used a very predictable, methodical vacuuming pattern. Then, when she was finished with the area beside Kyle's bed, Mother pushed the machine a few extra times for good measure. That's when it hit Emily's hip.

The vacuum cleaner paused, then Emily heard a click and wheeze as the machine ground to a halt. From beneath the bed, Emily watched Mother's knees and then her face appear.

"Emily!"

Emily didn't say anything. What *could* she say?

Mother said simply, "Emily. Come down to my room." Her voice was level, like a robot's. Then Mother unplugged the vacuum cleaner and pushed it out into the hall. She didn't wait for Emily but kept right on going downstairs.

Emily knew this didn't look good. She didn't feel it was such a bad thing to snoop in guests' rooms. What was the difference, really, between that and looking inside someone's picture window at night? But it seemed unlikely that Mother would see it in the same way.

Lately Mother seemed frayed, ready to break.

If Mother cracked, what would she do? Would she yell? Would she cry? Would she go crazy? It was frightening to think of Mother out of control. Emily didn't want to see her like that. That's why she had avoided Mother all week. But now a confrontation was inevitable. Emily walked into Mother's room. She took small, gentle steps as if she were walking on ice, as if the slightest sound would ricochet into the peaks and cause an avalanche.

Mother was standing at the window, facing Emily. Her face looked very old. It sagged like melting plastic. She lowered herself slowly and painfully to her mattress. She sighed deeply. She sat there, her arms hanging at her sides, and looked at Emily as if she were a stranger.

Emily sat down in the brown foamy chair beside Mother's bed.

"Emily, I did the best I could with you. I don't suppose I've been a very good mother, not young and fun, the way you'd like me to be. But Emily, I've always been here when you needed me. I've given you a home and I've taken care of you." Mother's eyes were desperate, begging. "I *have* taken care of you, Emily."

"I know, Mother."

Mother sighed. The air came out in jerks. "The

thing is, Emily, I don't know whether I can do it anymore. I work so hard that at the end of the day all I can think about is going to sleep. Then when I get to bed my dreams are busy, full of all the things I have to do the next day. And no matter how hard I work, there are always dirty clothes or dirty dishes or hungry guests and dusty rooms. And I just can't keep up." Mother put her damp face in her hands. Her wedding ring was twisted to the inside and the stone pressed on her cheek.

"I'm sorry."

"What do you have to be sorry about? I work so we can have a life. What choice do I have? What choice does anyone have?"

Mother pushed her bottom lip between her teeth. She held it tightly for several seconds.

"But Emily! Breaking into a guest's room!"

"I said I'm sorry."

"Is it a cry for attention? Is that it?"

"No."

"Because if it is, Emily, I just don't know where I'm going to find the time or energy." Now Mother's voice sounded small and far away, like she was speaking from the bottom of a deep well. "I don't have any more to give."

Then silence. Silence was worse than talking.

It was worse than anything because you never knew what came after silence.

Mother looked so weary. She looked like she had lived a hundred years. Emily wanted to reach out to Mother, to reassure her, but her hands would not move. She didn't know what she could say. It made her uncomfortable to think of comforting her own mother. Emily thought of the girl who had made the fantasy scene. Now this girl was Mother, beaten and weary. How does a girl like that become a woman like this? Is that what happens when you grow up? Emily felt sick, like she wanted to throw up. Would she turn out like Mother, too?

Emily walked out of Mother's room quickly, silently. She walked through the living room. She did not answer Kyle when he called, "Hi, Emily! How have you been?" There was only one place Emily wanted to be now.

At first it had disturbed Emily to see Bruno like this—muddy, his feathers scruffy with birdseed stuck to them. But she was used to it now. The big bird looked over his beak at Emily. She had jammed her hands in her pockets and was squeezing her jacket closed from in there. Bruno honked softly and backed up. He waited for Emily to crawl into the cage, but she did not. She re-

into something small. Maybe that explained Mrs. Sharples' tight, mincing steps. Also, she probably wore a full slip with adjustable straps. As a general rule, ladies who call their purses "pocketbooks" wear that kind of slip.

With luck, she wore dentures. She did have straight, even teeth, too perfect to be real. Emily thought if nothing else, something could be done to her dentures or maybe her denture powder. That is, if Emily could ever get into her room.

Emily wasn't absolutely committed to the denture thing. She wanted to leave her options open. When Emily got into Mrs. Sharples' room she intended to snoop around for something really embarrassing or incriminating. But it was unlikely that Mrs. Sharples had ever done something incriminating. She was a "talker," not a "doer." Even though gossiping could be as evil as many crimes, it was not against the law. That's why the denture thing was so perfect. Doing something to Mrs. Sharples' dentures would be like melting the pistol of Al Capone. The Sharpleses were leaving on Sunday. This was Emily's last chance.

"Ernie, sweetheart," Mrs. Sharples said at breakfast, "let's us two lovebirds take a little walk after breakfast."

mained outside, kneeling, clutching the edge of the cage with her fingers. She knelt there a long time before she said, "Do you remember your father, Bruno, and do you miss him? Probably your father flew away with your flock. Maybe someday you'll see him again. Maybe you'll be swimming on a lake and all of a sudden there he'll be. But Bruno, that will never happen to me. My father is dead."

Bruno held very still.

"It was a motorcycle accident. He was riding without a helmet. The rescue squad said he was already dead when they got there. He died so quickly he didn't give anyone a chance to save him. He didn't even say good-bye, Bruno. He left me! And *he didn't have to die!* If he'd worn a helmet, Mother said, he would have been okay. He would have been hurt but he would be alive!"

Hhnonk. Bruno settled into his feathers.

"Why didn't he wear a helmet?"

Bruno popped back up.

"Now I don't have a father and everything is different! Mother can't handle it and neither can I!" Emily was yelling. Screaming! She surprised herself with the sound of her voice. It didn't seem like it was coming from her. Part of her brain was rational and had separated itself from Emily's body. Now

this rational part floated somewhere above Emily and looked down on this hysterical person.

"She's a little worked up," explained the rational part.

Emily's hand bunched into a fist. *"I hate him for dying! I hate him!"* she screamed.

"She's had a hard day. That, and the grief," said the rational part.

"Life is so damn shitty!"

"Swearing is a device for venting her anger. It will help get it out of her system."

"Shit shit shit shit shit!"

"Now that she's expressed her anger, she will begin the healing process."

Emily reached into the deep corners where her anger had hidden for so long, and cried.

CHAPTER EIGHT

Snooping on Mrs. Sh

Saturday
1. *Get into Mrs. Sharples' room*
2. *Get into Mrs. Sharples' room*
3. *Get into Mrs. Sharples' room*

So far, Emily hadn't been able to snoo Sharples' room. Nonetheless, there we things she'd figured out by watching instance, Emily could tell that Mrs. Sha with foam rubber hair curlers, because blippy little sausage curls clamped d shiny line. The curlers were probably reddish-brown stain from her hair dye

Emily also knew Mrs. Sharples' shoes small. Her feet puffed out around the h edges, a sure sign of jamming someth

Ernie had thin lips. Lizard lips. "Whatever you say, darling," Ernie mumbled into his muffin.

This was Emily's chance! She flexed her hands underneath the table, wriggling her fingers with anticipation.

Breakfast was nice. There were oatmeal muffins with raisins, Emily's favorite, a cheese omelet, and pineapple juice.

After breakfast, Ernie brought down Mrs. Sharples' pocketbook and coat. He held her coat out for her as she jammed her arms into it. She reached in her pocketbook and took out a compact. She snapped it open and looked at herself in the mirror. Her lips parted in a grimace as she dabbed at a bit of smudged red lipstick with a tissue. Emily noted, with satisfaction, her white, even teeth. The inn door closed behind them. Mr. and Mrs. Sharples were off.

They were unlikely to take a very long walk— how far can you go in tight shoes? So Emily raced up the stairs, taking two at a time.

"Emily!" called Mother.

Emily paused on the second floor, her foot in the air. "What?"

"I hate to bother you," came the voice from downstairs, "but I need some help in the kitchen."

Emily drummed her fingers on the banister.

"Sure, Mother. I'll be down in five minutes. I just have to—uh—do something for Miss Thomas."

"How thoughtful, Emily. Go ahead. Finish your errand and then come down to help me."

Emily raced to the little table in the hall. She opened the drawer and pulled out the duplicate key for Room 5, a plastic bag, and a shaker of baby powder. Her heart pounding, Emily walked silently to Room 5, slid in the key, popped open the lock, and opened the door to the Sharpleses' room.

First, a quick once-over through the oak wardrobe. Emily flung open the doors soundlessly and began a methodical search of the clothes inside. She plunged her hands into each of Mrs. Sharples' pockets, looking for anything unusual—the phone number of an illicit lover, an address of a sleazy bar, a matchbook from a topless joint. She found several tissues with lipstick prints on them from when Mrs. Sharples blotted her lipstick. She found an appointment card from Colleen's Coiffures. She found a linty piece of gum. Emily arranged the clothes exactly as she had found them, and closed the wardrobe door.

Then she checked out the suitcase. Mrs. Sharples' underpants were flesh-colored and saggy. They were so big Emily could have worn them

mained outside, kneeling, clutching the edge of the cage with her fingers. She knelt there a long time before she said, "Do you remember your father, Bruno, and do you miss him? Probably your father flew away with your flock. Maybe someday you'll see him again. Maybe you'll be swimming on a lake and all of a sudden there he'll be. But Bruno, that will never happen to me. My father is dead."

Bruno held very still.

"It was a motorcycle accident. He was riding without a helmet. The rescue squad said he was already dead when they got there. He died so quickly he didn't give anyone a chance to save him. He didn't even say good-bye, Bruno. He left me! And *he didn't have to die!* If he'd worn a helmet, Mother said, he would have been okay. He would have been hurt but he would be alive!"

Hhnonk. Bruno settled into his feathers.

"Why didn't he wear a helmet?"

Bruno popped back up.

"Now I don't have a father and everything is different! Mother can't handle it and neither can I!" Emily was yelling. Screaming! She surprised herself with the sound of her voice. It didn't seem like it was coming from her. Part of her brain was rational and had separated itself from Emily's body. Now

this rational part floated somewhere above Emily and looked down on this hysterical person.

"She's a little worked up," explained the rational part.

Emily's hand bunched into a fist. *"I hate him for dying! I hate him!"* she screamed.

"She's had a hard day. That, and the grief," said the rational part.

"Life is so damn shitty!"

"Swearing is a device for venting her anger. It will help get it out of her system."

"Shit shit shit shit shit!"

"Now that she's expressed her anger, she will begin the healing process."

Emily reached into the deep corners where her anger had hidden for so long, and cried.

CHAPTER EIGHT

Snooping on Mrs. Sharples

Saturday
1. *Get into Mrs. Sharples' room.*
2. *Get into Mrs. Sharples' room.*
3. *Get into Mrs. Sharples' room.*

So far, Emily hadn't been able to snoop in Mrs. Sharples' room. Nonetheless, there were a lot of things she'd figured out by watching her. For instance, Emily could tell that Mrs. Sharples slept with foam rubber hair curlers, because she had blippy little sausage curls clamped down by a shiny line. The curlers were probably pink with reddish-brown stain from her hair dye.

Emily also knew Mrs. Sharples' shoes were too small. Her feet puffed out around the hard leather edges, a sure sign of jamming something large into something small. Maybe that explained Mrs. Sharples' tight, mincing steps. Also, she probably wore a full slip with adjustable straps. As a general rule, ladies who call their purses "pocketbooks" wear that kind of slip.

With luck, she wore dentures. She did have straight, even teeth, too perfect to be real. Emily thought if nothing else, something could be done to her dentures or maybe her denture powder. That is, if Emily could ever get into her room.

Emily wasn't absolutely committed to the denture thing. She wanted to leave her options open. When Emily got into Mrs. Sharples' room she intended to snoop around for something really embarrassing or incriminating. But it was unlikely that Mrs. Sharples had ever done something incriminating. She was a "talker," not a "doer." Even though gossiping could be as evil as many crimes, it was not against the law. That's why the denture thing was so perfect. Doing something to Mrs. Sharples' dentures would be like melting the pistol of Al Capone. The Sharpleses were leaving on Sunday. This was Emily's last chance.

"Ernie, sweetheart," Mrs. Sharples said at breakfast, "let's us two lovebirds take a little walk after breakfast."

Ernie had thin lips. Lizard lips. "Whatever you say, darling," Ernie mumbled into his muffin.

This was Emily's chance! She flexed her hands underneath the table, wriggling her fingers with anticipation.

Breakfast was nice. There were oatmeal muffins with raisins, Emily's favorite, a cheese omelet, and pineapple juice.

After breakfast, Ernie brought down Mrs. Sharples' pocketbook and coat. He held her coat out for her as she jammed her arms into it. She reached in her pocketbook and took out a compact. She snapped it open and looked at herself in the mirror. Her lips parted in a grimace as she dabbed at a bit of smudged red lipstick with a tissue. Emily noted, with satisfaction, her white, even teeth. The inn door closed behind them. Mr. and Mrs. Sharples were off.

They were unlikely to take a very long walk— how far can you go in tight shoes? So Emily raced up the stairs, taking two at a time.

"Emily!" called Mother.

Emily paused on the second floor, her foot in the air. "What?"

"I hate to bother you," came the voice from downstairs, "but I need some help in the kitchen."

Emily drummed her fingers on the banister.

"Sure, Mother. I'll be down in five minutes. I just have to—uh—do something for Miss Thomas."

"How thoughtful, Emily. Go ahead. Finish your errand and then come down to help me."

Emily raced to the little table in the hall. She opened the drawer and pulled out the duplicate key for Room 5, a plastic bag, and a shaker of baby powder. Her heart pounding, Emily walked silently to Room 5, slid in the key, popped open the lock, and opened the door to the Sharpleses' room.

First, a quick once-over through the oak wardrobe. Emily flung open the doors soundlessly and began a methodical search of the clothes inside. She plunged her hands into each of Mrs. Sharples' pockets, looking for anything unusual—the phone number of an illicit lover, an address of a sleazy bar, a matchbook from a topless joint. She found several tissues with lipstick prints on them from when Mrs. Sharples blotted her lipstick. She found an appointment card from Colleen's Coiffures. She found a linty piece of gum. Emily arranged the clothes exactly as she had found them, and closed the wardrobe door.

Then she checked out the suitcase. Mrs. Sharples' underpants were flesh-colored and saggy. They were so big Emily could have worn them as bloomers. It made Emily feel one-up on Mrs. Sharples to know what her underpants looked like. Now, whenever Mrs. Sharples said something terrible about Emily, Emily could picture her wearing those hideous, saggy things and feel better.

Mrs. Sharples' makeup case held three tubes of blood-red lipstick, face cream . . . and the treasure Emily had hoped to find: powdered denture adhesive.

Denture adhesive made dentures stick in your mouth. Emily had seen the commercials where denture wearers could eat an apple or talk with friends with confidence when using denture adhesive. She figured a mixture of half adhesive and half baby powder would do the trick. Mrs. Sharples would sprinkle the powder on her dentures as usual, wet it, and insert the dentures. They'd stick . . . for a while. But then, maybe when Mrs. Sharples was laughing and her mouth was gaping, her dentures would fall down—*splot!* Maybe they'd even fall out of her mouth and everyone would stand there, first looking at Mrs. Sharples' teeth on the floor and then looking at her naked mouth. Emily hoped she would be there to see it.

Emily shook about half of Mrs. Sharples' denture powder into a plastic bag and slipped the bag into her pocket. Then she shook an equal amount of baby powder into the jar. She was mixing the combination when the door opened.

"Young woman!" said Mrs. Sharples, pointing a finger at Emily.

Emily was so startled she threw up her hands, sending the baby powder/adhesive mixture high into the air in a powdery cloud.

Achoo!

"My . . . my . . . my—*achoo!*" sneezed Mrs. Sharples. "My God! You've been going through my things—*achoo!*—you little juvenile delinquent."

Emily tried to imagine Mrs. Sharples in her saggy underpants, but that didn't make her feel better. Mrs. Sharples grabbed Emily's shirt sleeve, scraping her fingernails into Emily's arm and pulling her roughly.

"See here, young woman! What were you doing with my powder?" Mrs. Sharples grabbed the jar and held it to her own nose. "This smells . . . like perfume! You've tampered with it, haven't you? What did you put in here?" Mrs. Sharples took Emily by the collar and shook her. "I said, 'What did you put in here?' "

"Baby powder," whispered Emily.

Mrs. Sharples stood there with her mouth hanging open. If only her dentures would let loose now. A small laugh escaped from Emily before she had a chance to stop it.

"How dare you laugh! We'll see what's funny now." Mrs. Sharples' voice was cold and steady. Her eyes were narrow with revenge.

"Come along." Mrs. Sharples dragged Emily by the collar down the stairs. Emily felt sick to her stomach.

"Mrs. Crockett!" Mrs. Sharples called in a loud, shrill voice.

"I'll be with you in a minute, Mrs. Sharples," came Mother's voice from behind the kitchen door. Soon the door swung open and Mother walked out, wiping her hands on her apron. "What can I do for you Mrs. . . .

"Emily!" Mother stopped and stared at Emily, attached to Mrs. Sharples' fist. "What's going on here?"

"I'll tell you what's going on, Mrs. Crockett. Your daughter gained entry to my room. She went through my private property . . ."

"Emily!"

"There's more." Mrs. Sharples sniffed righteously. Her lips were tight. Her red lipstick made a bloody slash across her face. "In addition to the other transgressions, your daughter tampered with my personal hygiene items, adding foreign material to one of them, perhaps dangerously."

"Oh, Emily," said Mother.

"I want retribution," insisted Mrs. Sharples.

"Yes," said Mother.

Emily felt like she was choking. She wriggled uncomfortably, trying to get a little room between her neck and her collar. Mrs. Sharples tightened her grip.

"Let her go, Mrs. Sharples," said Mother weakly. "I'll take care of this."

Mrs. Sharples held on, now directing her anger at Mother. "I warned you, Mrs. Crockett. Your daughter is a juvenile delinquent. I'll give you a piece of advice." Mrs. Sharples jabbed a finger into Mother's chest. "The sooner you control this child, the better. She needs strong discipline. Spare the rod, spoil the child."

Mother said, "Thank you, Mrs. Sharples, for your concern. And now, if you'll excuse me, I'll discuss this privately with Emily."

Mrs. Sharples let go of Emily and walked off, muttering to herself.

CHAPTER NINE

Has Mother Cracked?

Emily sat on the brown foamy chair in Mother's room. Things had been a little better between Mother and her. But now . . . Why had she done it? It was so dumb.

"Emily," began Mother, "what were you trying to do?"

"Mrs. Sharples is such a jerk. She's such a mean old busybody, always talking about people, making them feel bad. I just wanted to make her look stupid. I wanted to pay her back."

"People like Mrs. Sharples are their own worst enemies. Don't you think everybody knows she's awful?"

"Maybe."

Mother said, "Tell me exactly what happened."

"I was looking in Mrs. Sharples' room for some evidence, something that would make her look bad. If I had found something like that, I wouldn't have done anything else."

"What, exactly, did you do?"

"I was pretty sure she wore dentures. Her teeth are so white and even, not like regular teeth."

"Yes . . ."

"I found her denture adhesive and I mixed in some baby powder." Emily looked at Mother. Mother's hand was up to her face. Her shoulders were shaking.

"Go on," Mother said. Her voice was high-pitched and uneven.

"I thought when Mrs. Sharples used the denture powder mixture it would hold her dentures for a while, and then when she laughed or something her dentures would fall out! But then she came in while I was mixing the denture adhesive and the baby powder. She said, 'Young woman!' and she scared me and I threw my hands up with the powder mixture. There was powder all over and I was sneezing. Then she grabbed me!"

Mother's shoulders were shaking. She was crying into her hand.

114

"I'm sorry, Mother!"

Mother's sobs were getting louder. "Mother! Really! I'm sorry!"

Mother said, "Denture adhesive and baby powder?"

"Yes."

Mother took her hand away from her face to reach for a tissue. Tears were streaming down her face—tears of laughter! She was laughing, not crying. She was laughing huge, shaking laughs that made her face red.

"Oh, Emily!" Mother tried to say more, but she was laughing too hard and she couldn't push the words out.

Emily had never seen Mother like this!

"Are you all right, Mother?"

"Yes! I *am* all right!" Mother pulled out a fresh tissue and blew her nose. She wiped her eyes, crumpled up the tissue, and left it on her bedside table.

"Emily, what you did was very funny but it was also wrong. You should not search guests' rooms and you should not tamper with their things."

"I know."

"So you'll have to apologize to Mrs. Sharples."

"Mother! I'd rather die."

"There's no other way, Emily."

Emily waited for a few minutes in case Mother changed her mind. When she did not, Emily walked out of Mother's bedroom. She would apologize to Mrs. Sharples, but she would do it her own way.

Mrs. Sharples was reading the *Door County Advocate* in the living room. She snapped the paper when Emily entered the room and lowered it, folding it slowly. There was a smug look on her face that made Emily's stomach boil.

"Mrs. Sharples," said Emily, picturing Mrs. Sharples in her saggy, flesh-colored underpants, "I've learned my lesson. I will never put baby powder into someone's denture adhesive, no matter how mean they are, and no matter how much they gossip about other people. I apologize."

Mrs. Sharples' face reddened and her jaw dropped open. Emily didn't wait around for Mrs. Sharples to accept her apology. She ran outside.

"Ernie! Ernest Sharples!" Mrs. Sharples' voice clanged through the inn. Ernie was practicing his golf swing outside. Mrs. Sharples rapped on the window. "Ernie, get in here," she shouted. "Pack our things this instant."

Then a miracle happened. Ernie did not get inside that instant. He took another golf swing. He took a nice, easy backswing and, on the descent, whacked the stuffing out of the Wiffle ball.

Rap rap rap!

"I'll be in soon, my pet." Ernie teed up another Wiffle ball and smacked it again. Then he noticed Emily sitting beneath a tree. He winked at her.

Emily took out her notebook and wrote: *"There is more to Ernie Sharples than meets the eye."*

Emily walked to the storage shed, picked up the cutoff milk carton, and plunged it into the seed bag. She let the seed fall back into the bag. She scooped it up, released it, scooped it up, released it. Then she walked to Bruno's cage. Bruno's feathers were gummed up with birdseed. She didn't like to see him so messy. Emily wished she could give him a bath, but she knew Bruno wouldn't let her handle him yet.

"Bruno!"

Hnonk.

"Hi, yourself, big guy." Emily squatted down and leaned against the side of the cage. "Mother's been acting so weird, Bruno, I don't know what to make of it. Before, there was always one thing I could count on, and that was Mother. She was always the same: careful, old, responsible. When Daddy was alive, it was like we were the kids and Mother was the parent."

Bruno paced back and forth at the end of the cage, plopping his feet softly against the cement floor. *Hnonk.*

"Thank you. Anyway, Mother and I have never been what you'd call close. But still, if things got crazy, if bad things happened, I knew Mother would be there to help me. I never had to worry about things. It was nice, in a way, to be able to count on her."

Hnk hnk.

"Maybe it was too much for her, I don't know. I suppose everybody has a limit and maybe she reached hers. But mothers shouldn't have limits. They should be able to handle whatever comes along, don't you think?"

Honk.

"Anyway, she started acting different, weird. She started laughing more and palling around with some of the guests."

Hnk-a-hnk.

Emily lowered her face into her hands. "Bruno, I'm only a kid! I shouldn't have to handle Daddy dying and then Mother acting different! It's scary, Bruno, because I'm not sure what it means."

Honk.

"See, first there's this kid-Mother, the one who made the fantasy scene and had a ballerina doll. Then there's this old-person-Mother, the one I've always known. Now there's this other-Mother. How do they go together?"

Bruno shook his wings out. Emily noticed some of the feathers were broken. They didn't use to be broken. What happened?

"Come along, Ernie!" Emily heard Mrs. Sharples—she could hardly miss it!

"I've got to go, Bruno. I want to see this." Emily crawled out of the kennel and walked unobtrusively to the parking lot. Mrs. Sharples was charging toward the car. Ernie was dragging all their paraphernalia: skis, a suitcase, poles. No wonder the man was so small. He was constantly being crushed.

"*Try* to keep up, dear," said Mrs. Sharples.

But the skis were sliding apart. Suddenly, the whole thing let loose. "Blanche . . ."

Emily scrambled for her notebook. She had to get this down. *Blanche!* It was perfect.

"I'm doing the best I can." Ernie winced, waiting. He was waiting, no doubt, for an explosion from Mrs. Sharples. Sure enough.

"Ernie, don't be such a wimp! I'm losing my

patience. Get those things into the car." Mrs. Sharples tapped a foot impatiently.

"Of course." And Ernie did. He unlocked the trunk and scrambled back and forth, jamming their things inside.

Emily wrote: *Some things never change.*

After everything was packed up, Mrs. Sharples turned to have one more look at the inn. She scanned the yard, looking for something. She spotted it: Emily.

"You've had a little fun, haven't you, missy? You think you've been pretty clever. But let me tell you, you've tricked no one but yourself."

Then Mrs. Sharples pinched her lips together. She spun around and began to walk toward the car. That's when Emily noticed the toilet paper, stuck to the heel of Mrs. Sharples' shoe. She was trailing a piece of toilet paper, and she didn't know it! Mrs. Sharples got in the car, slammed the door, and squealed away.

Sunday

1. *Feed/water Bruno.*
2. *Sweep out old straw, put in new.*
3. *Item #7 in attic.*

This is weird, but I miss Mrs. Sharples. She's the kind of person you love to hate.

Bruno stopped waddling and stared at Emily; then he started pacing again. Bruno's behavior gave Emily a spooky feeling. Emily poured the seed into Bruno's dish. She sat in the corner and Bruno waddled slowly toward the food. He bent his neck and stared down at the food, but he would not eat it. Suddenly Bruno looked toward the sky. A small flock of geese was flying overhead. Bruno plunged upward, flying into the chicken wire, bumping his head and the arch of his neck.

"Bruno!" Emily cried. "Bruno, stop!"

But Bruno would not. He flew up and fell down again and again, crashing, catching his beautiful wings in the chicken wire, ripping out the feathers. Finally spent, he dropped to the floor of the cage and huddled against the mud and birdseed.

"Oh, Bruno," Emily cried, her voice catching on his name. Tears filled her eyes and spilled down her cheeks. Bruno wanted to go! He wanted to join the flock!

Emily bit her lip till it hurt and brushed the tears away. "Bruno, this is your home now." She had saved Bruno's life! She loved him. Bruno was hers to keep. If she let him go, maybe he'd get tired again. Maybe a new flock wouldn't let him in. Bruno was getting used to her. Soon he wouldn't miss other geese anymore. It would just take a little more time.

But Emily couldn't bear to see Bruno like this, so she left the kennel and walked up the porch steps toward the attic.

CHAPTER TEN

Letting Go

Emily groped for the light string. There. She pulled it and the light went on. The attic was familiar to her now, but today it felt different. It seemed charged with something, like the air before a storm. Emily closed her eyes, spun around, and walked until her foot bumped into a box. The box was labeled "Agnes—size 12." Emily knelt next to the box and tore off the old masking tape.

Inside were clothes—dresses, skirts, blouses. Everything looked plain. Of course, fashions were different thirty years ago. Still, these were pretty ugly clothes. They must have been ugly even then. Emily pulled out a pair of brown oxford shoes. They were badly scuffed and clunky. Poor

Mother! There was a navy-blue jacket at the bottom of the box. The jacket wasn't so bad. It had brass buttons. There were large flap pockets, and Emily noticed that one of the pockets bulged a little. She felt inside and pulled out a book. A diary.

Emily sat cross-legged, surrounded by Mother's clothes. The cover of the diary was red leather with gold lettering. There was a little clasp that held the pages shut. When Emily slid the closure, the clasp sprung open.

The name page said:

The Diary of:
Agnes Thorgeson

Emily began to read.

February 18.   Agnes is a name that smells like boiled cabbage. It's an old lady's name. When I have a little girl I will give her a beautiful name.

February 19.   Aesop and I played Davy Crockett today. Aesop was a bear who became my trusted companion. When Far saw me with my coonskin cap, he said I shouldn't play make-believe. He scolded Mor for letting me waste my time and said I should be practicing my arithmetic. Mor said she didn't know I was playing, she thought I was doing my homework. Far said she should keep better track of me. When they started quoting scriptures I snuck away.

April 27. Emily is the most beautiful name in the world. When I have a little girl I'll call her Emily.

May 14. Aesop died. Mor says that life and death are God's will. Mor says I must learn to accept it.

May 21. I sleep with Aesop's dog cushion every night. It makes me feel like he's closer.

June 5. Finally Mor let me go to my first movie. I went alone. The movie was *Old Yeller*. It was great! Old Yeller was brave and he reminded me of Aesop. After the movie, I put my ticket stub in my jacket pocket to save.

Emily looked in the other flap pocket. The ticket stub was still there!

June 14. I saw Judy Kagen in town today. When I crossed the street she hurried into the dime store. I think she saw me.

June 21. I cut a hole in the attic wall with Far's saw. It took a long time. I'm going to make a secret world in the hole. While I was in the attic I heard Mor calling me. I didn't answer.

June 22. I cut a stream for my secret world. When I covered it with plastic it looked like real water.

July 9.   Some Chicago people took my picture today. They said I was "quaint."

July 11.   I finished the caterpillar tree house today. It was a million degrees in the attic!

July 21.   We had meat loaf and boiled potatoes because today is Wednesday. I asked if we could have mock chicken legs tomorrow, like Judy Kagen's family. Mor said, "No, because tomorrow is Thursday." On Thursday we always have potato soup.

September 5.   There was a package on my bed. Inside were two bras. I tried one on and it felt like a horse's harness. I'm not going to wear it.

September 24.   I found Far's old elastic bandage from when he sprained his wrist. I wrapped it around my chest to stop it from growing.

October 12.   The girls at school act funny in front of boys. They swish around, hoping the boys will notice them, and when they do, the girls laugh behind their hands.

October 15.   We played baseball at recess. I was the last one chosen again even though I can hit the ball as far as Kathy Gunst. I wish I could make the other kids like me. I wish I had a best friend.

October 29.   Far caught me reading *The Wizard of Oz* today. He said I was "filling my head with nonsense." Then he threw the book in the garbage—and it was a library book! He said I was too old to read fairy tales, and from now on I will have more responsibility in the business. He said when I finish high school I will take over the bookkeeping position. I said I didn't want to, that I wanted to be a librarian or a foreign journalist. He said I was impertinent and walked away.

October 30. Mor said it was decided. I have to be Far's bookkeeper.

November 9. Today is my birthday. I'm 13. A teenager. Mor said I'm a young woman now and I must put all childish things aside forever. I DON'T WANT TO GROW UP! I REALLY DON'T!! If I could stop myself from growing, I would. Does every teenager feel this way?

November 21. I went to the store and bought a bag of miniature marshmallows. I hid them in the attic.

December 1. I took a mug of cocoa up to the attic today. It was cold up there and the warm cocoa tasted so good. I put some of my little marshmallows on top. Cocoa with marshmallows is my favorite treat!

December 12. Mor found my marshmallows today. She was putting something away in the attic and she found the bag. She got so angry! She said the marshmallows could have drawn vermin. She said it was deceitful to hide things. She said I shouldn't have wasted my money on such foolishness and if I had money to waste then I should start paying my way around here.

Emily sat very still for a long time, the diary in her hands. Vivid images and thoughts washed through Emily and she did not stop them. She let them come and go. She was touched by them and moved by them. Finally, when they faded, she was ready. Emily drew in a long breath and let it out very slowly. Then she went to Bruno.

"Bruno," she said, pressing her face to the chicken wire, clinging to it. "Remember when you came, tired and hungry, and I took care of you? I thought I had saved *you*! But Bruno, you were the one that healed me. Now I know that."

Softly, "*Hnonk, hnonk.*"

"Bruno, I wanted you to live here forever. I wanted us to be friends—and we are, aren't we?"

Honk. Yes!

"But Bruno, it hurts so much! I didn't know it would hurt so much!" Tears stung Emily's eyes.

"Will you remember me?"

Honk. Yes!

"Oh, Bruno!" Tears spilled out of Emily's eyes and ran down her cheeks. Emily swung the door wide. But Bruno didn't understand. So Emily shooed him out. "Go, damn it, go!"

Bruno gathered up his rear end and waddled away, toward the open door. Even outside he didn't seem to understand. He hovered on the other side, just outside the doorway. Emily waved her arms. "Get out of here! Go!"

Then they heard the honking. It came closer. When the flock was near, Bruno swung back on his legs and pushed upward. He bent his neck, anticipating the crash at the top of the cage. When it didn't happen he paused in the air, confused. At last he understood. He was free!

Emily watched through blurry eyes as Bruno flapped his wings, shaking off the bits of seed and mud, eager to shorten the space between him and the flock. He rose more quickly now, honking steadily, until he was where he was supposed to be—part of the flying wedge.

Emily reached her hand to the sky and touched the part where Bruno flew. Long after the flock had disappeared, Emily watched the empty sky. Then she sank to the ground. It felt as if Bruno had reached into Emily's chest and taken her lungs away.

Suddenly Mother was kneeling on the frozen

ground, reaching for Emily, gathering Emily up in her arms as if she were a tiny child. She held her tenderly, as if she might break, as if she had.

Emily said, "Mother, I *had* to let him go."

"I know," Mother said, holding Emily more tightly. "I know."

Then Emily cried—huge, gulping cries that tore at Mother's heart until Mother's tears mixed with Emily's. Then they cried, Mother and Emily together.

Emily said, "I've never done anything that was so hard to do. Will it stop hurting?"

"Someday it won't hurt so much." Mother smoothed Emily's hair away from her forehead. "Losing someone, saying good-bye, always hurts."

"I wish I didn't love him so much!" Emily could still see Bruno flying away.

"Emily, you can't hurt unless you love. And now I know you can't love again until you've hurt. So if hurting is the price you have to pay to love again—and sometimes it is!—then we have to pay it because there is nothing so dear as loving someone."

Emily asked, "Mother, did you love Daddy?"

Mother sighed deeply. "I loved him more than I knew. It's been difficult for me to lose him, and it's been hard to take care of so many things without him." Mother reached into her apron pocket, pulled out a tissue, and began to wipe away Emily's tears.

That night, Emily could hardly sleep. Whatever sleep she found was fragmented and fitful. Outside, dark clouds that had hung suspended for two weeks at last pushed in on themselves, gathering strength.

At first, just a few flakes sifted down, but before long the snow was tumbling furiously. It was heavy and wet. It clung to the trees and bushes. It covered the rooftops, the lawns, the fields, the roads. It made sharp edges white and soft.

When Emily awoke Monday morning, she immediately sensed the shimmering brightness. She drew the bedspread-curtain aside and pulled in her breath. It was magnificent!

Quickly she dressed and ran outside, eager to join the others for breakfast. She wanted to hear voices and see faces lit with excitement. She wanted to see Mother.

The inn was warm. It had the peculiar smell that comes when a furnace has had its first real heating challenge. In the living room, Sara Mueller was talking with Mr. Fredrich. Her hands were wrapped around a coffee mug. She bent toward Mr. Fredrich, her face flushed with excitement. She looked, Emily realized with a rush, almost beautiful. Mr. Fredrich's eyes were twinkly and warm. His bald spot glowed with reflected light from the window.

"Emily!" called Ms. Mueller. "Good morning!"

"Hi, Ms. Mueller."

"Well, well, well. This snow sure is something, isn't it? Eight inches, I'll betcha," said Mr. Fredrich.

"I'll bet that means *someone* doesn't have school today," said Ms. Mueller. She emphasized someone the way nurses, teachers, and old people do. She was such a stitch!

"Maybe not," said Emily. She looked outside again, squinting into the brilliant sunlight. The snow and high winds had drifted the road shut. The school bus could not get through. Emily had the day off.

"Have you seen Mother?" she asked.

"No, dear, I haven't," Ms. Mueller said.

Mother wasn't in the kitchen, either. There were a few baking dishes in the sink, soaking. Emily felt the water. It was lukewarm.

Emily found the sign in the dining room. It was taped to the wall over a large pot of coffee.

HELP YOURSELF TO COFFEE AND MUFFINS.
ENJOY THE DAY!

AGNES

Mugs and plates were set up, along with a basket of muffins.

Kyle and Beth burst through the front door, stomping their boots on the braided rug to release the snow. Bits of melted snow clung to Kyle's mustache. "Isn't this great, Emily?" said Beth, rushing over to Emily. "Don't you just love the first snow?"

"Yes," said Emily, "I do."

Then Emily heard it. It was a distant yell—a whoop, really, and laughing. Emily ran to the window and searched outside. She looked out over the yard and the hill beyond. When the red pomponned hat bobbed over the top of a hill Emily recognized it at once. Mother!

Mother, coated with snow, was pulling a sled! Never in her life had Emily seen Mother go sledding. Emily smiled when she saw Mother careen down the hill wildly, disappearing from sight.

Emily walked to the kitchen. She scooped one spoon of cocoa and two spoons of sugar into a cup. She added a little milk and stirred it into a paste. She poured in the rest of the milk and mixed. Finally, she put a handful of miniature marshmallows on top. Emily printed out a note.

MOTHER,
HELP YOURSELF TO COCOA.
JUST HEAT AND SERVE.

LOVE,
EMILY

P.S. I LOVE YOU!

Then Emily slipped on her jacket and mittens and stepped outside. The sun had gained strength through the morning, shooting flashes of light off crystals of snow and the dripping icicles that hung on the eves. It was so bright that it took a few minutes for Emily's eyes to adjust to the light. When they did, she noticed the footprints.

How funny. Emily had never paid much attention to footprints before. Maybe, in the city, there were too many. Maybe she had never really looked. It was fascinating the way they crisscrossed the landscape. Each set of footprints was a trail. Each started somewhere and ended somewhere. At one end was a person who used to be—a person who is, by the passage of time marked by the trail, different now.

Suddenly, Emily wanted to know who was at the end of the trails. She wanted to know who they were. She wanted to find them.

Emily scooped up a handful of snow, packed it into a ball, and threw it against a tree. It exploded there, leaving a white, powdery mark.

Emily chose one of the trails, hoping it was Mother's. She set off to follow it, to see who was at the other end.